Ghosts of Acadia

Marcus LiBrizzi

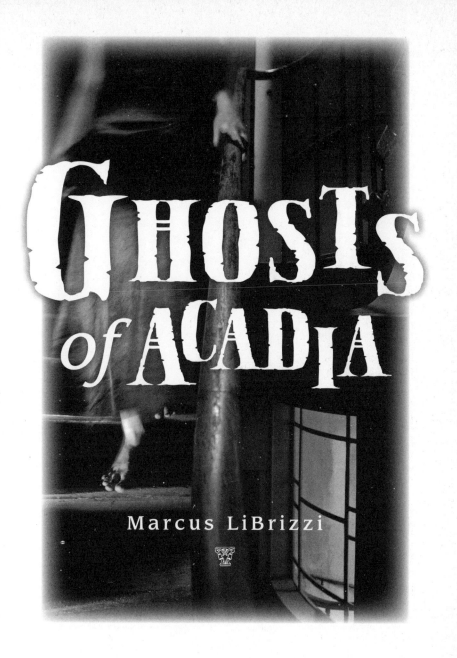

GHOSTS of ACADIA

Marcus LiBrizzi

Down East

ISBN 978-0-89272-921-0

Designed by Lynda Chilton

Printed at Versa Press, East Peoria, Illinois

5 4 3 2 1

BOOKS·MAGAZINE·ONLINE
www.downeast.com

Distributed to the trade by National Book Network

Library of Congress Cataloging-in-Publication information available
upon request

For Jacob, Tyler, and Ali

CONTENTS

1
PHANTOMS
of LEDGELAWN

Brooding over the village of Bar Harbor, Maine, stands a place of legendary proportions. This vast, sprawling structure goes by the name of Ledgelawn. With enough ghost sightings to fill an entire volume, Ledgelawn lives up to its reputation as the most haunted mansion on the island. Indeed, it casts a spell of darkness and horror to this very day.

The spectacular, shingle-style manor commands an oversized lot on the south side of Mount Desert Street, two doors down from the Church of the Holy Redeemer. Even the most casual passerby can feel a ghostly pall hovering over the old mansion. Built in 1904, Ledgelawn was one of the last of the true "cottages," an incongruous term referring to palatial estates built of simple bungalow-style elements such as cedar shingles. At one time Ledgelawn was the setting of lavish parties and balls, with candlelight and orchestral music spilling from the open windows and carriages lining the curving drive. At one of these events, the

Hope Diamond even made an appearance, glittering on the neck of an illustrious guest.

Long before the close of the town's Golden Age, Ledgelawn abruptly ceased its festivities. The fastening of a funereal wreath on the massive front door began a long era of doom and mystery. Yet the house survived the 1947 fire that destroyed so much of Bar Harbor—the unstoppable flames came within inches of Ledgelawn before something drove them away. The fire abruptly shifted direction, sparing the historic property. After functioning for decades as an inn, Ledgelawn came under the ownership of Ocean Properties in 2010. Although the great structure may not stay open to the public, it will always remain a landmark to the paranormal.

The most celebrated phantom of Ledgelawn is arguably its most sinister—a specter of a young dark-haired woman with madness in her smile. The story goes that a woman named Mary Margaret took her own life at Ledgelawn when her fiancé jilted her shortly before their wedding day. Mary Margaret possessed all that a person might desire—riches, youth, and beauty. Ironically, these gifts left her completely defenseless to the pain of a broken heart and the sting of public humiliation.

To the third floor of the mansion went the distraught girl, and in a sewing room on the east side of the house she found her wedding dress, hanging white and ghostly. Whether the sight of the dangling dress suggested the unthinkable, we'll never know, but what happened next is legend. Decking herself out in the wedding gown, Mary Margaret hung herself by attaching the long veil to the beams of the sloping ceiling. That is where her family later found her, a ghastly parody of the blushing bride. Mary Margaret's face was so bruised that she was nearly unrecognizable. The final horror was the grotesque smile twisting the blackened face of the corpse.

Since then, the specter of Mary Margaret has appeared on countless occasions. She looks almost as she did in life, young and lovely, except for the strange smile that distorts her whole face. The setting of the suicide became a guest room at the Ledgelawn Inn. People who checked into Room 326 were apt to wake up to the image of a woman in white floating in the moonlight at the foot of the bed. Or, as experienced by one guest, a phantom veil appears to sway all night from the sloping ceiling. Anyone inside the structure must beware since Mary Margaret freely walks the halls of the old estate, manifesting herself elsewhere in the dwelling, despite her odd attachment to the room where she died.

Some witnesses have heard the ghostly legend, but most have not and therefore arrive without preconceptions. In one instance, the ghost appeared to an elderly woman, Donna Gerda, who had just arrived from Brazil. Donna Gerda spoke only Portuguese, and she knew nothing of the house or its history. Yet on the morning after her arrival, she saw the apparition in all its classic form. As Donna Gerda was descending the grand staircase, she was in full view of the front desk, staffed by two employees, Jomar Castro and Sherry Gallant. They both saw her stop suddenly and begin waving her hand and nodding her head excitedly, but she wasn't looking at them. She was looking at someone that neither of them could see. When questioned later, Donna Gerda described seeing a young, dark-haired woman wearing a veil and a long white dress. Before disappearing, the phantom woman kept smiling up at Donna Gerda in a most disturbing fashion.

As a caretaker of the mansion for fourteen years, Mike Gallant has had his own unforgettable encounters with the unsettling wraith, but one instance stands out in particular. The event took place in October 2000, when Mike and the staff were shutting down the inn for the season. Nothing strange happened until the ghost cornered him upstairs. He had left the rest of the workers on the first floor in order to inspect the guest rooms above. Despite the fact that all the doors were open, and all the lights were on, a deep sense of gloom and confinement was building up inside the old manor house. Certainly, the darkness grew as Mike proceeded in his work—after he finished inspecting each room, he turned out the lights to indicate that the job was done. During this time, no one came upstairs past Mike, engulfed in the growing shadows of Ledgelawn.

When Mike climbed to the third floor, things really began to get strange. A light he had turned off in one room suddenly turned itself back on again. What happened next has etched itself permanently into his mind. He had just turned off the light for the second time, and he was leaving the room when a quickly moving object caught his eye. Swiveling in its direction, he faced Room 326.

He saw the white apparition of Mary Margaret slip out the door of an adjacent room and float across the corridor into Room 326. As the specter was passing by, she slowly turned her head around to make eye contact with the astonished caretaker, then flashed him a smile of fathomless intent. She was only ten or twelve feet away, so Mike got a good look. In his words, "it was as if time stopped when I looked at the object, and I began to focus, and in a split second realized I was seeing a woman in white smiling at me as she passed." It occurred to him that he was effectively trapped, for the hallway formed a *cul de sac*, with only one way in and out.

Ledgelawn is home to other phantoms. One of these is the spirit of a young woman who worked as a maid in the mansion years after it was sold by the original family. One morning, servants found this woman at the bottom of one of the back staircases. Her neck was twisted and broken. Rumor had it that someone pushed her down those stairs. Certainly, she had been uncommonly pretty, and in the whispered tales of the town, she was having an affair with her married master. Arguments ensued—and either the wife or the maid made implacable demands. Then all ended with a sudden death quickly hushed up in the interests of the wealthy owners of the estate.

The phantom maid manifests herself as a feeling of nameless dread, or the sensation of being watched when no one else is present. Commonly, the specter travels as a preternatural draft—ice cold on the hottest summer day—that snakes throughout the mansion. Other times, this vengeful ghost slams doors and echoes the sounds of a heated argument in rooms that are dark and empty. Her favorite place to haunt is a suite that once housed the separate bedrooms of the master and mistress of the manor. For years, each of these rooms contained an antique portrait—of a man in one room, and a woman in the other. On many different occasions, guests and staff at the hotel have been surprised to discover that the portrait of the man had been strangely altered during the night. In the morning the picture still sat behind glass, but only the back was visible in the gilt frame. Apparently, the phantom maid turned the picture around in a show of rage against her former master.

During a séance conducted in the mansion years ago, the presence of another ghost was reported, that of a young boy who drowned while visiting Ledgelawn with his parents when the place was still a private residence. While the boy did not die on the grounds, his frightened spirit apparently returned to Ledgelawn, where he still remains, hiding in the vast warren of Victorian cabinetry.

The specter of a lurking man stalks the servants' quarters of the cellar. This ghost appears as a silhouette or dark figure that shimmers like heat off the highway. There may yet be other phantoms at Ledgelawn, for the sprawling mansion sits on the site of an earlier house, built in 1876 on the actual foundation of a still older structure. As each house was torn down to make room for a larger one, Ledgelawn absorbed all their secrets—and all their specters.

And so Ledgelawn lives on—a stunning site of supernatural wonder. The shadow cast by this malignant mansion falls over the whole town. Contained within its labyrinth are the spirits of the unfortunate and the damned. Expect to encounter them yourself in the deep gloom of the place—a vengeful draft, the slamming of a door, a floating veil, and the apparition of a corpse bride with a smile reserved solely for you.

2
ACTS *of the*
UNSPEAKABLE

I magine the scene: The bell tolls off the shoals of Seal Harbor. The moon hangs full over the silvery waters of the Atlantic. Like a shroud, a low bank of fog creeps slowly over the Cranberry Islands and descends upon the land. On the sea cliffs near the Cooksey Drive Overlook the atmosphere begins subtly to change, and a darkness of utmost evil settles in with the fog and the damp smell of saltwater. Then comes the reenactment of one of humanity's worst crimes, an act of horror that has replayed itself here for more than two hundred fifty years.

The supernatural event takes the form of sounds out at sea. Moans and cries, faraway lamentations, and wailing sobs convey a sense of utmost suffering and despair. In the hold of a ghost ship that cannot be seen, hundreds of men and women cry out for their lives and their souls. Their cries for help go unanswered, for these are spirits doomed to repeat their final torment over and over again. The ghastly recital lasts as long as the sinking of the ship, and then falls a most terrible silence.

The story began in the late 1750s. Slavery was legal and no laws stood against the importation of slaves from West Africa into the colonies. Yet the British made restrictions—costly licenses for slave ships, as well as duties and taxes on their human cargo. Under these circumstances, a new breed of smuggler came onto the scene. Hoping to land a fortune, a young man from a prominent family entered upon a scheme with some companions. They planned on "running slaves." They would outfit a merchant ship as if it were heading out for a long voyage to the East Indies. In actuality, it was going to Africa to pick up slaves.

Many ships have been called the *Pride of the Seas*, but one in particular was most ill-suited for the name. This ship sailed from a port in southern New England, probably from Rhode Island, a major sector in the slave trade. Concealed within the hold were manacles and chains that could hold hundreds of men and women. Troubles beset the *Pride of the Seas* from the start. Just as it reached its destination in the Congo, a British warship sailed in range and signaled the *Pride of the Seas* to stop for customs and inspection. Only darkness and clouds aided the smugglers in slipping past the warship.

A couple nights later, the smugglers returned to make their devilish bargain. In a hidden cove, African slave traders had three hundred slaves penned in an enclosure. In exchange for boats and merchandise, the smugglers obtained all the slaves, stowing them aboard the ship so closely together that there was no possibility of their changing position or even lying down. As in other boats of this kind, slaves had as little as sixteen inches of floor space. There was no way even to remove the dead from their chains until the voyage was complete. Fortune seemed to shine down on the slave smugglers, celebrating upstairs in the captain's quarters, but little did they know what lay ahead.

On the return voyage, a whole set of complications ensued. Docking in the West Indies, the truth about the *Pride of the Seas* almost came under detection once again. To maintain the charade, and for purposes of piracy, the smugglers agreed to lead a convoy of merchant ships up to New York, rather than unloading the hidden slaves as soon as possible in the markets of the southern colonies. Naturally, the ruse only prolonged the agony of those stowed away below decks. Close to New York, the smugglers on the slave ship seized on their last chance to plunder the boats in their fleet. This reckless action proved to be a success. With hundreds of thousands of dollars in stolen money, the men aboard the *Pride of the Seas* needed a place to conceal their unexpected gains, and to decide what to do next. Only a short distance by sea, Mount Desert Island, then in a state of abandonment, offered the perfect hideaway. Legend has it that the *Pride of the Seas* and its convoy of stolen ships approached the island from the south, and anchored at Otter Creek.

There are different versions of the horror that took place. In every account, though, the *Pride of the Seas* sank with all its slaves still chained in the hold and crying out desperately for help. Meanwhile, the crew escaped in boats and didn't bother to look back. From here, the similarities stop. One version of the story has the ship going down in a gale. In another account, the smugglers accidentally ran the ship against a rocky ledge attempting to avoid detection by yet another British warship. The actual location of the wreckage is also a matter of dispute, but not for islanders, who know otherwise. For them, the slave ship went down in Seal Harbor, an opinion based on oral history passed down in the region for hundreds of years. Of course, Seal Harbor is right next to Otter Creek, where the slave ship anchored, and such a location does not lend itself to theories of an *accidental* shipwreck.

All of this brings us to the worst of all accounts. This is a tale of utmost depravity, in which the smugglers deliberately sank the *Pride of the Seas*, with all three hundred slaves on board. Supporting this horrifying outcome is the smugglers' piracy of the ships in their convoy. The slave dealers unexpectedly found themselves with much more wealth than they could possibly handle. The risks were now simply too great to return to the South as originally planned. The human cargo, already dying in the suffocating barrows of the ship, had become a liability. And so the slave dealers decided to cut their losses and sink the whole ship once and for all. This took place one foggy night in the nearby waters of Seal Harbor. This account was already long in circulation in 1883, when patrons of the *Mount Desert Herald* read that the captain of the *Pride of the Seas* "scuttled his ship and departed."

On one thing all accounts agree. The screams and cries of the drowning slaves haunted the smugglers to their end. As they rowed away from the doomed *Pride of the Seas*, the captain and crew heard the agonizing screams and shouts of the manacled slaves, and the terrible memory of those cries followed the men. As if in retribution, many of the smugglers met early deaths in the watery grave of the sea. Others went completely insane. No matter where they went, the wretched wailing followed them. Nothing, it seemed, could stop them from hearing the hopeless screams of the slaves chained to a sinking ship.

The story stands as a cautionary tale, not only of the depths of evil in the human heart, but also for the chances of hearing the ghosts of the drowning slaves. People can go to Seal Harbor as they have for centuries, and if the conditions are right they will hear carried over the water the screams, wails, and sobbing of the unfortunate spirits entombed within the ghost ship. Anyone who has heard their pitiful cries is haunted ever afterward by the memory of gloom, despair, and senseless evil that led to such inconceivable suffering. But for the ghosts of the slaves, the final horror is the continuation of their terrible plight. For these tormented souls, there is no relief in sight—not even in the misty realms of the afterworld. Indeed, they are condemned to reenact in perpetuity one of the great crimes of history.

3
HORROR *at* BASS HARBOR HEAD LIGHT

The lighthouse at the head of Bass Harbor is recognizable worldwide. Reproduced on millions of postcards, the white tower with its black lantern sits high atop pink granite cliffs over sunset waters. While Bass Harbor Head Light is certainly famous, few people know of its horrifying past or its history of ghostly visitations. The lighthouse has been the setting for murder, vengeful ghosts, and a former curse that once led to injury and even death. Bass Harbor Head Light is certainly a study in contradictions. Well known yet poorly understood, beautiful yet damned, the landmark stands for supernatural encounters that are truly strange—and dangerous.

The grounds of the lighthouse are open year-round from 9 a.m. to sunset, which is spectacular on this side of Mount Desert Island. From the very tip of Bass Harbor Head, fifty-six feet above high tide, the lighthouse looks out over the open sea and the islands in the Gulf of Maine. As the only lighthouse on Mount Desert Island, the place is very popular, averaging a thousand visitors a day during the summer. Out of respect for the privacy of Coast Guard officials living there, visitors are not allowed into the lighthouse, the attached keeper's house, or on the land immediately around these structures. Yet the trip is well worth making for both the breathtaking scenery and the possibility of supernatural encounters.

Blood baptized the building of Bass Harbor Head Light, leading to a curse that lasted more than a century. Construction on the brick tower and attached wood-frame keeper's house began in 1858. A certain number of men began work on the structure, and when they were finished, one man was missing. A search turned up an axe covered in blood lying on the rocks outside. Yet the missing man was never found or heard from again. A rumor soon began that he had been sealed into the structure of the lighthouse. Particularly around the base of the cylindrical tower, there are a number of dead-air spaces that could conceal a body. Renovations over the years have focused on the keeper's house, leaving the brick lighthouse untouched. Without a doubt, the killer must have premeditated the crime, working side by side with his intended victim all summer long in 1858. Having selected a place to conceal the body, the killer then seized on his last chance to carry out the bloody deed.

From its construction until the day of its automation in 1974, Bass Harbor Head Light has meant bad luck. Among the keepers who lived at the station, an extraordinary number of these people experienced personal tragedies. Phoebe Gray was the wife of one of the early lighthouse keepers. She died of a heart attack while living at the light. Charles Gillis, another keeper, died there in 1872, and later, keeper Eugene Colman suffered a terrible stroke. Willis Dolliver came to work at the lighthouse in 1894, never dreaming that his wife Barbara would leave the station in a casket. The wife of Elmer Reed also died while living at Bass Harbor Head Light in the late 1930s.

The old lighthouse became notorious for a deathly atmosphere thought to bring on disease and accidents. While June Noise was living there, she contracted typhoid fever, but fortunately she left in time and survived. Shirley Archileas was not so fortunate. She grew deathly ill when she came to live at the lighthouse, and she was so weak when she eventually left that she died soon afterwards. Leveret Stanley, one of the last civilian keepers, worked at the light from 1940 to 1950. While he was on a ladder repairing the structure, he took a debilitating fall. His wife Albra had already succumbed to a crippling disease, so that she could only walk about with the help of crutches. The two could barely leave the place they had come to in health and strength. Including the suspected murder that took place during construction in 1858, six people lost their lives in connection with Bass Harbor Light, while four more suffered devastating diseases or accidents.

If the spirit of the man entombed in the building was somehow responsible for the illness and death, then what was his motive? One possibility is that he desired to inflict his terrible fate upon the lighthouse keepers. The murdered man met his own end with the unexpected blow of an axe, and then, as legend has it, the killer sealed the body into the structure of the lighthouse. Immured behind bricks and mortar, the vengeful spirit could not wall up a living person, but the phantom might somehow bring about the death of that person's beloved partner. In this way, each widowed lighthouse keeper fell victim to solitary confinement out on Bass Harbor Head. Certainly, isolation was extreme at the lighthouse even in the best of times. Surrounded by thousands of acres of fir trees, the beacon was only accessible in the old days by poor roads and a difficult landing. Death drastically intensified this loneliness. Over and over again, the lighthouse keepers buried their spouses and returned alone to the outpost. For some of these individuals, life at Bass Harbor Head Light became a living hell. In a real sense, they felt buried alive, trapped inside the lighthouse that depended on their constant care.

Perhaps the specter's true intent was broader in scope, for the terrible curse ended only when the lighthouse became automated. Morton Dyer was the last civilian lighthouse keeper when he retired in 1957, but the lighthouse still depended on the care of a living keeper. Members of the United States Coast Guard lived at the station with their families and manned the light. But in 1974, the lighthouse became fully automated. Since then, Coast Guard families living there have been spared the deathly legacy of the place. This circumstance suggests that the phantom's real target was the safety of the ships that relied on the living keepers of the light to guide them safely into Blue Hill Bay. Through death and psychological torment inflicted upon the lighthouse keepers, the specter jeopardized their sacred duty to keep the lantern burning. While this evil spirit remains cloaked in mystery, his reign of terror has finally come to a close.

However, strange sightings still take place at the old lighthouse. Many people have seen a shadowy woman in a rocking chair. She appears in one of the windows of the keeper's house. Accompanied by a feeling of doom, this spirit remains a prisoner in the place that killed her. Other people have witnessed an apparition in the snow, an old man sitting on a stump during a snowstorm. Whenever anyone approaches the old man, he disappears, leaving no tracks in the snow. Local legend maintains that this is the spirit of keeper Charles Gillis.

But the mystery deepens. Some accounts describe a strange doorway to realms of the supernatural. One man saw a deer in a snowstorm that behaved in exactly the same manner as the apparition of the old man, disappearing in the blink of an eye and leaving no tracks in the freshly fallen snow. Also inexplicable are the strange sounds that people have heard over the years in the area. If such a passageway exists to other dimensions, then it's anyone's guess as to the true extent of the ghostly happenings at Bass Harbor Head Light. The spirits of people who died in the lighthouse are perhaps far outnumbered by the other strange entities that appear and disappear in the remote location.

Bass Harbor Head Light remains baffling, as well as terrifying, in terms of its paranormal past and the dangerous scope of its ghostly encounters. Perched above the waters of the Gulf of Maine, the lighthouse is one of few coastal stations still in operation in the United States. While the legacy of death has ended here, supernatural history still lives on at the strange outpost.

4
The SHORE PATH

Since 1881, the Shore Path in Bar Harbor has offered a beautiful walk easily accessible from the center of the village. Beginning at the town pier, the path follows the shoreline for more than half a mile along Frenchman Bay, offering breathtaking views of the Porcupine Islands, Schoodic Mountain, and the Black Hills. The Village Improvement Committee maintains the Shore Path, but it is the graciousness of private landowners that makes the trail possible. While the Shore Path is a cherished tradition in Bar Harbor, its heritage includes a long history of supernatural encounters. Indeed, the path presents a tour of haunted mansions and a walkway for strange phantoms.

The Shore Path starts out in the shadows of the Reading Room at the Bar Harbor Inn, a historic structure dating from 1887 that was originally a club for gentleman. As the saying goes, the only reading done at this club was through the bottom of a glass. Without a doubt, the place provided a place to escape Prohibition in Maine, which lasted nearly a century. Under the cover of a reading group, male visitors to Mount Desert Island could drink to their heart's content. The Reading Room, with its large glass rotunda, is now a restaurant connected to the Bar Harbor Inn. But two phantoms come from the early history of the place. These ghosts appear as two Victorian gentlemen sitting at a table by one of the windows. Be careful, if you see these specters, not to make eye contact. Doing so yields a deathlike chill that literally follows you.

As the path winds around Hardy's Point—still on the property of the Bar Harbor Inn—the trail crosses the territory haunted by the apparition of a forlorn woman. For centuries, this ghost has appeared at this spot, particularly at dusk. As darkness descends on the Shore Path, the atmosphere undergoes a complete transformation. Now the wailing cries of sea gulls and the rustling of leaves in the ocean breeze sound ominous. At this twilight hour, an apparition returns to stalk the shore. The ghost appears as a woman wearing a long cape. She stands, looking out across the water, or she paces back and forth over the worn rocks of the shoreline. Naturally, no wind stirs her cape or her hair.

According to local lore, this is the spirit of a woman awaiting her lover's return from the sea, but there is much more to this tragic story. The tale begins nearly a century before the Reading Room was built. On the Bar Harbor waterfront lived the Olsen family—a young couple and their infant son Luther. The father was a sailor, and the sea apparently claimed him, for he never returned from one of his long voyages. His young wife and child fell into great poverty, but at least they had each other.

When Luther was only five or six, he routinely combed the shoreline around Hardy's Point, collecting driftwood since he and his mother couldn't afford to buy firewood. Then one day, the young boy disappeared. People in the village thought he had been picked up and taken away by one of the ships, but the truth never surfaced. At any rate, Luther Olsen was never seen again, but for years his bereft mother was a figure of despair. She walked out every day to

Hardy's Point, watching for her lost son and husband. With her heart broken, she sank into an early grave, but her soul remains out there, condemned to wait in vain through the centuries.

Farther down, the Shore Path passes Albert Meadow, a park, and then Balance Rock. Seeming to sit precariously on the coastal ledge, this huge boulder was left behind by a melting glacier during the last Ice Age. Balance Rock inspired the name of the beautiful inn that stands nearby. The stunning property, which dates from 1902, has its own resident spirits and a history of hauntings going back for generations. Doors have a habit of opening and closing by themselves at the inn, and objects seem to move around by themselves in certain rooms. It is not uncommon to hear little footsteps running down empty hallways. Whether these incidents result from trickster spirits, or ghosts from a parallel time, no one can say.

In the late 1960s, when the Balance Rock Inn was still a private home, the Hutchins family lived there. Each still remembers paranormal occurrences that took place in the house. Bobbie-Lynn Hutchins recalls, as a girl, having the distinct feeling that a ghost was living in her bedroom. One night she learned that her ghost might be real. Bobbie-Lynn planned to sleep elsewhere for the weekend, and as she walked into her bedroom, she teased her ghost by saying to herself, "I'm not even going to be sleeping here, so the joke's on you." At that moment, her feet flew out from underneath her, and she fell startled to the floor. Bobbie-Lynn has excellent balance, and nothing like this ever happened before or since. Her sister Suzanne also had an encounter with a trickster spirit. She was walking down the second-floor hallway and distinctly heard something clap loudly right in front of her face. Yet she was all alone in the corridor.

Stranger still are sightings of phantoms at the inn. The figure of a minister sometimes appears facing a second-floor window, and people have heard his voice gently admonishing ghostly children who sometimes run laughing down the upstairs hall. Could this be the same apparition seen by residents of the property in the early 1980s, long after it had been sold by the Hutchins family? At the time, the figure of an old man was apt to appear walking about the mansion. One of the most remarkable sightings took place in the gardens overlooking the Shore Path. As Bobbie-Lynn and Suzanne remember the story, their father was mowing the lawn when he noticed a woman who appeared as if transported from the early 1900s. She wore a long skirt and a tall collar, and her hair was crimped. What stood out most, however, was the look of confusion, if not utter horror, on her face as she stared at the lawn mower.

Not far from Balance Rock, the Shore Path passes Devilstone, an estate partly dismantled in the 1960s. With Reef Point appearing in the distance, the path approaches the long breakwater that shelters Bar Harbor from the sea. According to local lore, J. P. Morgan built the granite barrier to stop the waves from rocking his yacht and spilling his guests' drinks. Nearby is a somber mansion notable for its size and style. The mammoth house looms right over the Shore Path, and unlike the shingle-style estates lining the trail, this mansion is built of stone and half timbers in the Tudor-revival style. Now known as Atlantique, the estate's original name was the Breakwater. The architect Fred Savage designed the mansion, built in 1904 for the great-grandson of John Jacob Astor. Builders spared no expense in the construction of the palatial residence, even adding secret passageways and a hidden staircase.

The Breakwater is arguably the most beautiful home on the Shore Path—and the most haunted. The great gloomy hall contains the spirits of former residents who insist on making their ghostly presence known. A dumbwaiter, now completely nonfunctioning and even covered up inside the house, sometimes acts on its own. From within the walls, the old elevator suddenly starts up, creaking as it makes its ascent or descent, carrying invisible contents summoned from another world. Different owners over the years have grown accustomed to hearing voices in empty rooms. The staff has a particularly difficult time keeping the mansion clean since the ghosts of the Breakwater continually leave their impressions. It is not uncommon for a housekeeper to make a bed and then turn away, only to turn back around to discover that it looks as if someone had just been lying on it, the covers unaccountably wrinkled and sunken. Indentations of invisible heads appear on pillows, and freshly vacuumed carpets reveal new footprints only seconds later. It's no wonder staff members are edgy and easily startled when working alone, for the signs of ghostly inhabitants are a continual reminder that the living share quarters with the dead at the Breakwater.

Crossing a little wooden bridge, the Shore Path comes to an end at Wayman Lane, which returns to the village. Truly, the path offers an unforgettable experience. As it winds along the rocky shoreline, the trail brushes past a remarkable number of ghosts, from the many spirits who refuse to leave the gilded mansions in which they lived and died, to the forlorn wraith of a bereft mother appearing over the centuries at Hardy's Point. The Shore Path provides a uniquely haunting experience, leading travelers on a tour of Bar Harbor's legendary sites of the supernatural.

5
SHADOWS *from* the FLAMES

Bar Harbor contains numerous signs of an enormous disaster from the past, the Great Fire of 1947. Gates that lead to nowhere and ruined towers reveal the locations of mansions scorched to the ground. Modern hotels appear on the sites of other burned estates, where only the granite roadside walls survive. Remains of the Great Fire are abundant here, but this event and other fires have left another kind of trace. Indeed, a supernatural legacy of horror hangs over the land. Among the victims of fire, phantoms stalk the shores, the streets, and the halls of the town.

The ghosts of the fire seem out of place in the sheer natural beauty of Bar Harbor, with Cadillac Mountain forming a grand backdrop and the Porcupine Islands dotting Frenchman Bay. From sparkling waters skimmed by sailing ships, yachts, and cruise ships come the cool sea breezes. Carried away by the wonders of the place, or the hustle and bustle of the village, we may never notice the sinister specters from the flames. These phantoms may be hard to detect, but look closely, for they are all around, and they might even be watching you.

A record drought followed by extremely high winds proved to be a lethal mix in October of 1947, when the Great Fire broke out. Strangely, the fire seemed destined to devastate the town, for three separate fires all started in the same cranberry fields, but it was only the last fire that raged out of control. The origin was the Crooked Lake Road in Hull's Cove, but the fire swept south into Bar Harbor and Acadia National Park. More than a third of the park and half of the town went up in flames while the National Guard worked with firefighters to control the blaze and evacuate citizens from the once-picturesque harbor. Months after the fire was officially out, the peat was still burning four feet below the snow in Sieur de Monts Meadow.

When all was said and done, the damage from the fire was staggering. Most devastating of all was the loss of life. Six people perished in the Great Fire—three people died in car accidents during the evacuations, two died of heart attacks trying to escape the inferno, and one man burned to death. Animals were scorched as well, including ninety thousand mice at Jackson Labs, and one cat named Seawater.

One of the most famous ghosts from the fire turns out to be the spirit of this black cat named Seawater. The animal belonged to an elderly man named Willie Cunningham. Willie and his pet lived on Forest Street, directly in the path of the raging fire as it swept across Kebo Valley. With minutes to spare, an evacuation truck rescued Willie and Seawater, and as he drove away, Willie Cunningham watched his little house suddenly burst into flames. In a moment of panic, Seawater sprang from Willie's arms and leapt from the truck. Seeing his beloved pet racing back to the burning building, Willie jumped from the truck to catch the animal. He was last seen running through the smoke-filled street. The evacuation crew had no choice but to leave the man. When the fire finally died down a week later, residents began returning to their homes. One of Willie's neighbors stopped by the ruins of his house and made a ghastly discovery.

Willie's charred bones were lying in a pile on the bank of a small stream that flows through a granite channel near the crossing of Forest Street and Eagle Lake Road. Grief-stricken and overwhelmed with horror, the neighbor knelt to the ground. The fire-blackened skull faced the neighbor, who began to feel as though the empty eye sockets were staring up at something directly behind him. Swiveling around, the neighbor noticed a black cat sitting atop the steep eastern embankment. The cat was looking down at the skull of Willie Cunningham, as if the two were in the midst of some dark form of communication. Although the animal resembled Willie's pet, a strange and terrifying transformation had taken place, and a look of the utmost evil smoldered in the cat's red eyes. Jumping up, the man chased the cat, which ran a short distance before dissolving into thin air.

Since then, the ghost of the cat named Seawater keeps popping up in Bar Harbor. Its favorite place to haunt is the gloomy stream near the ruins of Willie's house on Forest Street. The phantom cat appears on the hillside as well as the granite bank of the stream. At times the ghost cat manifests itself only as a reflection on the dark surface of the slowly moving water. The little stream disappears into a cement culvert, and the phantom cat ritually returns to that pitch-black interior, appearing as a set of glowing red eyes. At other times, the ghost of Seawater stalks the town, and people have seen the cat on the Village Green, on Albert Meadow, and even on rooftops. Until it abruptly disappears, the phantom always looks solid. But unlike a living cat, the dark specter always imparts an overwhelming feeling of inescapable doom.

In another home in the village, psychic disturbances result from a tragedy that took place in a house fire. After a whole family perished in their home, anything built on the spot seems to contain the ghosts of the former occupants. At any rate, the residents who now live there see a group of spirits that look like little shadows. Dishes have a nasty habit of shooting off the tables, and pictures come flying off the walls. The ghosts from the fire appear to be destructive, but far more frightening are the spirits' attempts to be constructive. It is not uncommon for the ghosts to pull down everything in the bathroom and then stack the items up into a kind of pyramid in the tub. The horror-infested house is notorious for electromagnetic disturbances—sharp ringing sounds on the phone, mechanical difficulties, and unearthly voices. Truly, the spirits' behavior compares with the frantic actions of people trying to evacuate a place—throwing together their possessions, calling for help, and panicking.

The spirits of two Victorian ladies make a strange pair of phantoms. These ghosts come from an era before the Great Fire of 1947. But as it turns out, Mount Desert Island has a long history of devastating fires going back for centuries. In terms of fire alone, the island has been scorched on countless occasions, leading Samuel Champlain in 1605 to call the place the *Isle des Monts Deserts*, the island of bare mountains. The ghosts in question manifest themselves as the voices of two women from the late 1800s. In the halls of different hotels, the spirits talk loudly in a bygone manner of speech, and—as if looking for a room for the night—the two specters drag along large steamer trunks. Whenever a person investigates, the hotel corridors are always quiet and empty.

In a séance once conducted in Cleftstone Manor, the ghosts communicated that they came from long ago and are condemned to eternal vigilance. For these ghostly ladies, their restless existence consists of ceaselessly traveling from inn to inn to prevent fire from breaking out and once again ravaging the town. Because so many guests encountered these spirits in the upstairs halls of Cleftstone Manor, the rumor started that the spirits belong to two women who died there in the Great Fire. This story is pure fabrication, however. Cleftstone Manor was actually one of the few mansions on Eden Street spared the destructive path of the fire. The ghosts appear to be friendly guardians, if not somewhat disturbing in their manic obsession with durning to death.

Next door to Cleftstone Manor stand the great arched foundations of Mizzentop, which burned in the Great Fire. Approximately twenty-five years later, a motel built on the site also burned to the ground. Strangely enough, history repeated itself again in 1994, when another hotel constructed on the remains of Mizzentop also burned down. It has since been rebuilt into a four-diamond facility, the Bluenose Inn and Spa. The abandoned ruins in the forest nearby are truly haunted by the fire that consumed them. The piles of granite and broken bricks sometimes give off the most intense smell of fresh smoke, as if the old staircases and stone balustrades are still burning hot although they have rested beneath moss and fallen leaves since 1947.

From the fires of Bar Harbor come a strange assembly of spirits inhabiting the twists and turns of this beautiful resort town on the coast of Maine. There are a number of unsettling dimensions to these supernatural tales—brutal death, uncontrollable forces of nature, and a terrible past that seems to repeat itself over and over. Sometimes dismissed as living animals, or late-night hotel guests, the phantoms from the flames continue to communicate anguish, urgency, and calamity.

6
A PHANTOM
in the TURRETS

A classic haunted mansion lies at the heart of this special tale. The location is the Turrets, a Gilded Age estate still standing on Eden Street in Bar Harbor. Everything about the place suggests a fairy-tale castle, yet a heavy gloom hangs over the mansion even on the brightest of days, an oppressive reminder of restless spirits. Indeed, the Turrets is infamous as the site of the "white lady." For decades, encounters with this specter have taken place with alarming frequency. Regarding the ghost, a number of things stand out, notably a love story and an unsolved mystery.

From its inception, the Turrets was designed to win the heart of a particular woman. Seventeen-year-old Lela Alexander was the toast of Bar Harbor in 1892. Remarkably beautiful and accomplished, she moved with ease through the glittering high society. She had secretly given her heart to a young man who had yet to make his fortune. As luck woud have it, another man named John J. Emery came on the scene. The aging soap manufacturer, who made millions in real estate and railroads, had just arrived in Bar Harbor when he was instantly captivated by Lela.

John Emery would have Lela by any means, and in his courtship he described the house he would build for her, a castle over the sea where she would live forever as a queen. Through the pressure of her mother, and the overwhelming temptation of fabulous wealth, Lela Alexander broke off her attachment to her first love and accepted John Emery's proposal of marriage. The couple announced their engagement, and Emery immediately purchased a lot on "millionaire's row" to build his young bride her dream house. Like a fairytale castle, the house would have towers and turrets and great stone battlements overlooking the sea.

The Turrets took two years and one hundred men to build. During this time, John Emery and Lela Alexander were on an extended honeymoon throughout most of Europe and Asia. Bruce Price was the famous architect who designed the mansion, with stonecutters dragging ton after ton of granite from Eagle Lake. Built on a knoll overlooking Frenchman Bay, the house once contained elaborate gardens and a walled park that created a sensation in their day. Guarding the front door was a priceless relic sent back by the couple from their travels—a Phrygian marble elephant from the palace of the King of Agra. By July 1895 the house was completed, and the couple returned in a triumph that was short-lived, for a strange gloom hung over the Turrets, an unaccountable darkness apparent from the start.

Perhaps the oppressiveness of the house came from its construction, more like a tomb or prison than a summer house. In addition to exterior granite walls that are two feet thick, the house contains a brick firewall a foot thick. Yet, for all that anyone knows, the mysterious darkness of the Turrets came from the very rock taken from Eagle Lake—or the very location on the coast selected as the site of the mansion. At any rate, the couple tried their best to brighten up the place, even having the woodwork painted white. Still, a heavy darkness hung over the castle. Flowers seemed to wither faster there than elsewhere, and maids had instructions to change each bouquet every morning.

After a long and eventful life, Lela Alexander returned to the Turrets to die. This took place inside the mansion during the summer of 1953. In Bar Harbor again, the elderly woman must have reflected back over her past and the choices she had made. By her own estimates, her life had been a dazzling success. One of her daughters became a Russian princess and another a French duchess, and Lela herself became royalty when she married the son of the Earl of Litchfield after Emery's death. She had seen and done more than most people could have dreamed, and she no doubt looked forward to a safe passage to the next world. Unfortunately, her soul may still be inside the Turrets. Trapped there, her spirit seems unable or unwilling to leave.

Since the death of Lela Alexander in the Turrets, people have reported seeing the apparition of a woman in white, a wraith seen mostly in the Great Hall of the castle. This huge room, with fluted columns and a Venetian carved ceiling, runs the width of the mansion, from the front door to the back terrace over the bay. Here phantom perhaps waits to escape her confinement. Yet, in most sightings, the ghost has strangely embraced her doom, and appears content to guard or even exult over the castle that imprisons her. From this perspective, the Great Hall is still the perfect place for the spirit to make her manifestations. The phantom woman appears ageless, neither young nor old, with features partially obscured by the light that comprises the body of the specter. Never leaving the Turrets, the ghost only hides and waits to come out every night when the castle is truly quiet.

During the years of its abandonment, the Turrets lived up to its reputation as a haunted house. After the Emery family sold the place in 1958, the Turrets became a bed and breakfast and then a monastery, and then it stood empty for a number of years. Only simple garden twine held the tall gates closed in front of the overgrown avenue that led to a crumbling palace. Among the young people who broke into the Turrets, an extraordinary number have had encounters with the specter of the white lady. For the phantom persisted in startling trespassers, first with muffled sounds upstairs, then with the sensation of a cold hand, and finally with glowing manifestations at the end of the Great Hall, or at the top of the main staircase. An exorcism was even held in the mansion in the 1960s, but with no success. In all accoûnts, the spirit drove off intruders more quickly than the police.

The white lady still presides over the Turrets, which has survived the ravages of time. In the late 1970s, the castle became the property of the College of the Atlantic, one the premier environmental colleges in the country. The structure was restored thanks to funds from the National Trust for Historic Preservation, private donors, and descendents of John Emery. The building now stands in fine condition, though under altered circumstances, with the grand rooms serving as administrative offices and classrooms. The damask and leather are gone from the walls, and no marble elephant guards the front door, but the building remains as one of the most important Bar Harbor mansions still open to the public.

To the present day, the specter of the white lady appears tirelessly in the shadowy castle that holds her soul. She is well known among students from the college. On countless occasions, this ghost returns to the Great Hall long after security has locked up the building. The front door of the mansion contains a glass window looking directly into the hall, and the ghost typically appears at the opposite end. The phantom favors a high-backed chair at the end of the Great Hall. This chair, with its sunburst design, leather seat, and arms of carved oak, has a regal element, and this is where the ghostly woman appears night after night, as if to signify her role as the queen of the castle.

While everything points to Lela Alexander as the source of the spirit in the Turrets, the truth remains a mystery. Some evidence points toward a malevolent force originally tied to the land on which the castle was built. This dark force might explain the gloom that always hung over the mansion. Right next door to the Turrets is Witch Cliff, the name of another private house now owned by the College of the Atlantic. This house, dating from the 1930s, gets its name from a particular section of the coastline on Frenchman Bay. Here a twelve-foot cliff contains a detached section of rock, allowing anyone to stand on the beach and remain almost completely hidden. Yet this rock bears no resemblance to a person, much less a witch.

No one knows the origin of the name of Witch Cliff, but the term appears to have been handed down from early settlement. The name probably refers to the spirit of a local woman suspected of witchcraft long before the Turrets was built. Could this be the phantom mistaken for the ghost of Lela Alexander? If so, this ghost story lends itself to the peculiar horror that comes from the complete unknown and the cruel twist of fate that turned a fairy-tale castle into a ghostly tomb.

7
The CREEPING
at SEAL COVE

A tale of dark powers and secret treachery, this story stands out for the subtlety of its horror. The original accounts never specify the exact time period, but internal references indicate the early part of the nineteenth century, probably the 1840s. Ghostly manifestations have been taking place ever since in the area of a ghastly event. The setting takes place near Seal Cove, on the western side of Mount Desert Island overlooking Blue Hill Bay.

The story begins in the lingering light of a summer evening. A woman we'll call Hannah was out walking with her children near Seal Cove. In the harbor they saw a mysterious ship silhouetted against the sunset and they stopped to speculate on the ship's origin and contents. Hannah and her children were not long in talking before one of them noticed a small skiff that had set off from the ship with a party of people. The little boat was heading for the most isolated and unsettled part of Seal Cove. Desiring a better vantage point, Hannah led her children to the nearby ledges of Butler's Hill, located about three-quarters of a mile up the coast from the head of Seal Cove. In a grove of spruces now occupied by the site of a modern house, the woman and children watched unseen as the strange drama unfolded.

Growing closer and closer in the dwindling light, the small boat finally landed near the base of Butler's Hill, out on one of the small rocky outcrops surrounded by little white dunes of crushed clam shells. A party of eight men and a woman came ashore carrying shovels and a large object. They had clearly agreed on their destination because all the participants acted with wordless understanding. Breathlessly, Hannah and her children watched as the group passed directly below.

The men were dressed as sailors, and the large object they carried looked exactly like a treasure chest. Even more fascinating, however, was the woman who walked with them. She was young and beautiful, with dark hair piled high on her head and hanging around her face in long snaky coils. She was dressed like a noblewoman in a sumptuous gown of stiff silk that trailed on the ground and whispered as she passed.

The mysterious group walked the beach for a short distance past Butler's Hill until they came to the lowest area, where two small streams trickle into the sea. Veering into the woods, the woman and eight sailors soon disappeared completely from the view of Hannah and her children. Something momentous—and something awful— was taking place, for a thick feeling of danger and dark misgiving settled in like the growing dusk. This sense of impending doom prevented the mother and children from following the procession to see where it would bury the large treasure chest. Conflicting emotions no doubt gripped them—the desire for instant wealth urging them to sneak into the woods, and the instinct of self-preservation keeping them hidden at a safe distance.

As they deliberated in hushed tones, Hannah and her children kept watch over the dark shoreline. Although it was getting late, Hannah didn't dare take her family home for fear of encountering the ship's party on its return. Her caution paid off because she later noticed shadowy figures emerging from the woods and heading back down the beach. At first it was difficult to see them through the twilight, but as the group passed the base of Butler's Hill, Hannah had no trouble making out the shapes. Seven sailors walked directly below, heading back to the small boat anchored on the shore. The men moved quickly, no longer encumbered by the heavy chest, and they hastily assembled in their boat and cast off for the ship, which had nearly dissolved into the darkness. There was no sign of the eighth sailor or the young noblewoman.

From the woods that swallowed up the woman and sailor, only ominous silence prevailed—no sounds or signs that anyone had passed that way. Murder hung in the air, and, frightened, Hannah and her children made the difficult trek back home, stumbling in the dark along the rocky shore and doused by ocean water as they stepped accidentally into tidal pools. Long before they got home, the mysterious ship had pulled anchor and quietly departed, for the foreign vessel was long gone by the first light of morning.

The story quickly passed the rounds of Seal Cove about the sailors who buried treasure on the island and killed a man and a woman to guard it. Their deaths had been terrible acts of betrayal involving a strangling-cord that cut off any cry for help and a dagger to the heart. Into the hastily dug pit that contained the treasure chest, the seven sailors lowered the bloody corpses of the sailor and the woman, binding their spirits to the place. The treacherous sailors then filled the gravesite with rocks and sod, scattering moss and leaves to hide the spot. A fierce summer storm further camouflaged the site. Although people searched the area after hearing Hannah's tale, no one ever discovered the location. The murderous sailors never lived long enough to return and claim their hidden fortune. Perhaps an early death was the price of their crime.

For nearly two hundred years, the spirit of the murdered noblewoman has haunted the coastal wilds of Seal Cove. No one knows why only her soul remains out there, yet certain features stand out in the original account. The woman's death represented the darkest twist of fate, for she had walked into a trap having all the advantages the world can offer. Her youth, beauty, and social station all stood at the brink of unimaginable riches. Only at the moment of death did she learn the price for this fortune. Unable to come to terms with her bitter end, she must have died rooted to the very spot of her undoing. Since then dozens of people have experienced the ghost at that particular low spot near Butler's Hill where the two gloomy brooks flow into the sea. In the vicinity of the second stream lies the territory of the ghost.

Through this dismal spot, the strange phantom moves in a disturbing fashion. The ghost takes the form of a peculiar sound and sensation. Many people have heard the swish of a silken gown as the ghost approaches. Now a lonely dirt road crosses both the bubbling stream and a small swampy hollow of birch and alder trees growing in the shadows of Butler's Hill. In this remote location, a perpetual ocean breeze keeps the leaves in constant motion, creating a rustling sound much like crinkling silk. Sometimes the water, trickling over moss-eaten stones, makes a similar sound. Truly unsettling is the great number of snakes that congregate in this particular lowland. The slithering of these reptiles among the grass and fallen leaves only adds to the strange whispering in the haunted glen.

While the sounds of water, leaves, and snakes certainly lend themselves to the legend of a creeping specter, these noises cannot explain the paranormal intensity of the site. Interspersed between the noises of the natural environment comes the sound of something else, the slow approach of the phantom. Difficult to perceive at first, the ghost's movements seem to come from far away. Then, unexpectedly, you will hear with perfect clarity the swish of a silk dress trailing on the forest floor. Looking around, you'll see nothing. Nonetheless, the ghost seems suddenly much closer. When the sound returns, the rustling comes from a different direction, but always closer. In this way, the ghost creeps in a roundabout manner. With one or two steps followed by a stop, the specter keeps closing in.

While the ghost's motives remain baffling, its approach certainly resembles a predator stalking its prey. As the specter circles in, the creeping becomes intolerable. With darkening intensity, the phantom inspires a cold dread. Then, when the silk gown rustles close by, you will know the dead woman is standing directly behind you. You must flee the haunted glen before the ghost touches you. A sense of danger guides you, prompted by a sudden insight. The ghost guards a treasure, and the only way to that fortune is through death itself.

8
The SINISTER WEB of 1613

One of the most enduring ghost stories of Acadia concerns the spirits from its very first European settlement, a doomed colony of French Jesuits. These forlorn spirits stalk the southwestern shores of Mount Desert Island. The ghosts of the dead Jesuits manifest themselves in a secret grotto, a bewitching spring, and in the deep shadows of Flying Mountain and Saint Sauveur. While the tales themselves are disturbing, there is a deeper source to the dread they inspire than the spirits of the murdered Jesuits. Indeed, these ghost stories form only the nucleus of a maze of terror stretching across the whole island. In this strange set of circumstances lurks the true center of horror.

The short-lived settlement once stood on Fernald Point, in Southwest Harbor. Seen from above on Eagle Cliff, located on Flying Mountain, the regions below glisten like paradise—green points of land, stark blue water, mountains plunging into the sea, and the vista of Somes Sound, the only natural fjord on the East Coast of the

United States. This deep ocean channel was cut during the last Ice Age by an enormous glacier, almost slicing the island in half.

In the spring of 1613 a ship called the *Jonas* set out from France, carrying forty-eight passengers. Among them was a group of young Jesuits hoping to start a religious colony in the New World. Their destination was Kenduskeag, Maine, on the Penobscot River. Blinding fog in Frenchman Bay, together with a fateful series of events, induced the young missionaries to found their city of God at the head of Somes Sound on Mount Desert Island. They called the place Saint Sauveur.

In their idealism, they neglected to build fortifications or make any plan for their defense. The first thing they did was build a chapel, and lovely indeed must have been the sound of the bell ringing that first morning. The Penobscot Indians, living across the narrows in Northeast Harbor, came with as much curiosity as good will. Close ties of friendship were soon formed.

Into this utopia, an English warship arrived late in the summer. The captain of the ship was a deceitful and bloodthirsty man named Samuel Argall. He had sailed down to Acadia specifically to obliterate any attempts at French settlement. Seeing the Jesuit colony, he bore down on its ship anchored at the head of the Sound. The small crew of men on board hardly had a chance to send out a sign of friendly welcome before the English warship attacked. The English ship of one hundred thirty tons was manned by sixty men and armed to the hilt. There was no question as to the outcome. The craft raced down on the *Jonas* and unloaded fourteen guns in a shower of cannonballs and grapeshot.

When it was over, eight Jesuits had died of wounds or drowning. Some of the wounded French hid in a secret grotto previously shown to them by the Indians. This remarkable cavern on Fernald Point has an underwater entrance, but leads up to an air-filled cavern at the base of Flying Mountain. There, the wounded died, already entombed within the enclosures of the earth. Others fled up into the mountains, only to give themselves up later because they were starving. Survivors from the ill-fated colony were sold into slavery, or cast adrift on the open ocean. Some dead bodies were placed in unmarked graves on Fernald Point. The godless Argall even went so far as to burn the cross from the Jesuit chapel.

The tormented spirits of the murdered Jesuits haunt the region, and offer a solemn warning to all who encounter them. These ghosts appear in the deep shadows of Flying Mountain and Saint Sauveur Mountain, at the Abbe's Retreat, and sometimes in Gold-Digger's Glen, leading to the theory that fleeing Jesuits buried the treasure supposedly located there. The place most haunted, however, is Jesuit Spring, located two thirds of the way down Fernald Point.

Spellbinding and inaccessible, Jesuit Spring lives up to its reputation as a place of enchantment. Out of a crag in the rocks of the beach, flows a pure stream of freshwater. This spring spills over a little beach of silver sand and crushed shells that sparkle underwater when the tide is high. Despite its beauty, people rarely visit the place. Islanders avoid Jesuit Spring, knowing that boats docked there have a habit of completely disappearing. Other strange things have taken place as well. Many people have heard the sounds of men praying in French accompanied by the splashing of oars. People sometimes see the apparition of a murdered Jesuit holding a cross and looking up with imploring eyes.

At other times, the whole spring turns red, a ghastly river of blood. Tradition holds that the Jesuits haunt this spring because they were buried nearby, or perhaps killed here. Another possibility concerns a fabled ring supposedly lost in the vicinity. A Jesuit named Gilbert du Thet received the ring from the French noblewoman who financed their expedition. This Templar ring was made of gold and contained a carnelian stone the color of blood. In a popular novel from the 1800s, someone finds the ring, but no one has ever discovered the real object, if indeed it truly exists. This fabled treasure is rumored to contain intense supernatural powers.

Without a doubt, the most frightening aspect to the Jesuit ghost stories is their prophetic quality. "As it was in the beginning, so shall it be in the end" goes an old saying, which applies to these tales, for they form a legacy most monstrous, not about the past, but about the future. This is because the destruction of the first European settlement foreshadowed so many disasters to come. Over and over again in the history and lore of Mount Desert Island the terrifying face of destruction returns to wipe the place clean. The Great Fire of 1947 was only the last of these cataclysmic happenings.

In a certain sense, the dark pattern of circumstances points to the possibility that the whole place is cursed. Over the centuries, fire has scorched the island again and again, but this was only one of many forms of destruction on Mount Desert. Warfare was mostly responsible for causing the complete abandonment of the place between 1700 and 1765, although Native Americans had occupied the island for thousands of years. In one of the great unsolved mysteries of history, a search party of one hundred men vanished without a trace in the fall of 1739. Smallpox and other diseases decimated the place, and an outbreak of cholera in 1873 almost snuffed out Bar Harbor's tourist industry in its infancy. Meanwhile, the island experiences tremors and earthquakes, as if to signal more upheavals to come. Native American lore is replete with dark supernatural entities from *Pemetic*, the original name of Mount Desert Island. In a certain sense, these terrifying phantoms give a face to a much more ancient and mysterious force of destruction.

And yet, Mount Desert still shines as one of the most beautiful places on earth. Could it be that the natural beauty masks the island's truly dark and destructive side? If so, then we are no different than the French Jesuits, so captivated by the wonders of the place that they never foresaw the dangers around the bend. Even the name of their boat, the *Jonas*, was ill fated. On their arrival in Frenchman Bay, the Jesuits were met with several other warning signs never taken seriously. For a long time they were lost in a fog so thick they could see nothing, though they knew deadly rocks stood nearby.

When the fog finally lifted, a dreadful scene appeared before them. The *Jonas* first landed in Compass Harbor, where the Jesuits saw smoke from Indian fires, and they heard from the beach a commotion of wailing sobs and cries of grief. A funeral was taking place, the very first thing the French Jesuits saw on Mount Desert—clearly another bad omen. The overcast skies only added to the melancholy gloom shrouding the coast. Later that day, across the island, the sun broke from the clouds and showered gold upon the mountain valley by the sea. Venturing forth into this earthly paradise, the Jesuits forgot their original trepidations. And the rest is history.

Like wheels within wheels, the Jesuit ghost stories of 1613 draw in many of the legends and accounts of the supernatural on Mount Desert Island. What frightens us most about the ghosts is the bleak warning they have to offer. As if to alert us to a danger lurking unseen, these dark-robed phantoms keep appearing, century after century! Yet their solemn message goes unheard.

9
WITCHCRAFT
at SOUTHWEST HARBOR

W ho hasn't fallen under the charm of Southwest Harbor? The stunning views of Somes Sound framed by mountains and the white sailboats gliding across the Western Way captivate the imagination. Delighted by the cries of gulls, we never heed the warning call of the owl hidden on the wooded shore. Dazzled by the sunlight on the waves, we do not notice the shadows that have gathered here for centuries. For who could dream of secret horrors festering within this pretty village? Yet the lingering spirit of a shapeshifting witch still haunts Southwest Harbor. It is the ghost of Sally Somers, out and about, and larger than life, casting her spell of appalling darkness.

Sally Somers was the daughter of a medicine woman who lived on Fernald Point in Southwest Harbor in the late 1700s. Sally's mother, Elsie Somers, possessed great magical powers. She chose Fernald Point for its mystical properties as the greatest psychic portal on the whole island. For the same reason, Native Americans occupied the site centuries earlier. The place is awash in magical qualities. On the summer and winter equinox, the shadows of Dog and Flying mountains converge on the same place on the peninsula, and near this site, Sally and her husband built their homestead. The house was perched on the very vortex of the supernatural.

Around the house grew a garden of strange proportions. When Elsie Somers had moved from Connecticut, she brought with her a vast collection of clippings, seeds, and root material. These she planted in strange configurations around the house, her choices dictated by planetary alignments. From this immense garden, she concocted tinctures and salves and a host of other strange potions. For the most part, Elsie used her powers for good purposes. She made medicines to heal the people in the area in both body and spirit.

Owing to her supernatural abilities, Elsie Somers enjoyed the tribute of all the shipping in Southwest Harbor. No vessel bound up Somes Sound would pass her place on Fernald Point without bringing her a "gift." These offerings of tea, pork, or rum guaranteed the boats a safe voyage. Woe to any captain who neglected this rite of passage. Many stories circulated of ships cursed by Elsie Somers because they refused to pay homage. One tale concerned a sea captain who scoffed at the whole idea, only to run aground soon after on one of the points in the mouth of the Sound. For days he toiled with his men, but the boat was hopelessly lodged. At last, Elsie appeared and offered to float the vessel for a round of pork. As soon as the sea captain relented and paid the dues, he found his boat floating free and clear.

Elsie's daughter, Sally Somers, chose the dark side. And it is, unfortunately, the spirit of this dreadful woman who still stalks the byways of Southwest Harbor. Sally Somers was born on Fernald Point on April 24, 1791. Early on, she inherited her mother's psychic powers, plus easy access to the mysterious gardens and the library of ancient spell books. A pall of darkness gathered around the black-haired girl. Using witchcraft, Sally lured a young man named John Clark into marriage. He walked about as if frozen in a trance, but sometimes he would break out of the spell. Then, in stark-eyed terror, he would try to escape the clutches of his bride and her strange family. John Clark disappeared one night right before he was secretly bound for a distant shore.

Sally's powers of darkness included the ability to send out her spirit in different forms. Taking the shapes of animals, her spirit stalked the town, and no lock could keep her out. These black animal spirits looked strange indeed, for they all possessed Sally's eyes, and nothing reputedly could kill the infernal creatures. Most dreaded of all were the phantom hounds. In one of her rituals of satanic witchcraft, Sally sacrificed two black dogs at the top of Dog Mountain, which earned the prominence its name for centuries—it is now called Saint Sauveur Mountain. On the basis of this horrendous ritual, Sally Somers took on the ability to send out her spirit in their form—as the hounds of hell—and in these shapes she terrorized the region, even drinking blood.

But Sally's favorite form to take was that of a black cat. This feline possessed great intelligence and a truly strange set of eyes for a cat. With preternatural ability, the cat could show up anywhere—in the barns and bedrooms of the village—until it came to be a source of dread and pandemonium. Numerous times frightened villagers shot the cat, but always it escaped safely in a black streak of shadow. In the meantime, troubles grew. People who spoke out against Sally had to take great care that her animal familiars were not lurking nearby listening, for then an unfortunate series of freak accidents always ensued, sometimes dragging people to the grave.

Sally Somers finally met her own end. A neighbor remembered that a silver bullet was supposed to kill witches and other entities that possess the ability to shapeshift or send out their spirits in different forms. As in legends of the werewolf and the vampire, silver alone can kill what other metals leave untouched. Melting down a coin of the realm, Sally's hateful neighbor fashioned a single bullet sometime in the year 1832. When the phantom cat next appeared, the man shot the special bullet directly into the animal and instantly killed the cat. Legend has it that Sally was in her home at the time and cried out, "They have killed my cat." She took ill, and three days later she was dead.

While Sally's body now rests in an unmarked grave in the Gilley Burying Ground, the woman's spirit is free to terrorize the region. In the house where she once lived, strange things still take place. Remnants of the vast medicinal gardens still exist in the form of a huge apple tree and some herbs and currants from the days of Elsie Somers. While this woman sought to heal people, her daughter's evil spirit has seeped into the ground and poisoned the plants and trees from the original herbarium. Anyone who eats of this fruit today, particularly the apples, will soon after sicken, suffer an accident, or die.

Knowing the history of the house, Daisy Harper was worried about the safety of her mother, who worked there in the summer of 2004. One day, Daisy decided to leave an offering to appease the spirit of the old witch. The daughter made a gift of colored stones, which she planned to leave near the old apple tree. Between the trunk and the branches of this monstrous tree, Daisy discovered a large crack, and into this hole she dropped her offering. Strangely, the little package took an extremely long time before it hit bottom, and by then the sound of impact was very, very far away. Could the apple tree be growing over the gateway to another world?

People report the sensation of being watched inside the house. The pieces of furniture have a habit of moving by themselves, in the night, or when the place is empty, sometimes leaving scratches on freshly polished floors. In the dining room, windows overlook the head of the Sound and the village waterfront. Tradition has it that anyone who breaks a pane of glass in this room will be the next to die. In one of the wavy panes of glass there is a most remarkable formation. An imperfection in the glass bears a striking resemblance to a witch. The weird figure even appears to be sitting at the edge of the sea. The image is a clear reminder that the spirit of Sally Somers is still around.

As for the ghost of the witch in her animal form, no one recently has reported seeing the phantom hounds. However, the ghostly black cat has shown up numerous times over the centuries deep inside the shadowy forests on Saint Sauveur and Flying mountains. The black cat with its human eyes is particularly fond of the dismal glen near Man-of-War Brook. The haunted reputation of these woods even stunted the development of hiking trails in Southwest Harbor during the nineteenth century, when people were more apt to shun the hills because of the ghostly occurrences that took place there with alarming regularity. The whole area is no less mysterious today. And so lives the spirit of Sally Somers, and her longstanding access to strange and forbidden powers.

The BAR HARBOR CLUB

Darkness gathers at the Bar Harbor Club. This historic property stands on West Street overlooking Bar Island. The restoration of the Bar Harbor Club is truly impressive, from the gas lights at the covered entranceway to the hand-carved staircase in the front hall. But gilding and polishing cannot wipe away a history of injustice, horror, and mystery. Along with beautiful views and a palatial facility, the Bar Harbor Club contains a native terror.

Certainly, the old club has left behind a ghostly trace of dazzling wealth and shameful elitism. The groundbreaking ceremony took place in 1929, on the eve of the country's worst financial crisis, yet the club still opened its doors the next July, in a grand opening of festivities that included a lavish costume ball inspired by *The Arabian Nights*. The club offered the best in swimming and tennis on the island. From a balcony over the vast pool, musicians played chamber music while waiters served patrons and doormen kept everyone else out. Some of the country's wealthiest families belonged to the

Bar Harbor Club, but no amount of money could buy a membership. One had to be nominated by two members and then go through a screening process. Only rich, white Protestants need apply.

For years the Bar Harbor Club stood out as the most haunted place in town. The building certainly looked like the set from a horror film. In ruins, the club sat empty for nearly two decades. After the Great Fire of 1947, the character of the resort town changed for a time, but the club limped on bravely, growing more tattered and faded until it finally closed in the late 1980s. Although purchased in 1992, the club was not renovated and reopened for thirteen more years due to zoning disputes. Eventually, the old club was reborn in 2005, more opulent than ever, its gloomy Tudor-revival style even spilling over into the massive new Harborside Hotel and Marina next door. Lovely as it is today, the Bar Harbor Club still retains its ghostly atmosphere in the minds and memories of town residents who recall its long days of abandonment.

Tales of murder have certainly darkened the aspect of the old place. When it was empty and in ruins, the club was often the setting for underage drinking. A hole in the chain-link fence near the sand bar gave anyone access to the confines of the wildly overgrown property. From there, intruders ventured up past the miasma of the old pool to the crumbling clubhouse. Through its many windows and doors, entrance to the dusty place was easily attained. Inside, trespassers sometimes experienced ghostly encounters in the deep shadows of the place. Vandalism rarely took place, but in the whispered tales of the town, an act of murder occurred in the building during this time.

The story goes that a young woman snuck into the clubhouse one day. No one knows whether she went into the building with her killer, or whether she encountered that individual somewhere inside, such as the mirrored ballroom. At any rate, the woman died by strangulation. The killing took place in the women's restroom located off the front hall of the club. No one has ever been able to substantiate this tale, yet the story is also difficult to disprove. The killer got away with murder, for there was never a police investigation. The killer apparently removed the body at night and buried it somewhere nearby on Bar Island. As the legend goes, the woman was wearing a perfume that lingered for a long time after the killer removed the body from the room where she died.

Since then, the spirit of this unfortunate woman returns to haunt the Bar Harbor Club. She manifests as the scent of the perfume she wore on the night she died. This fragrance will unaccountably show up in the marble restroom off the front hall and the Vanderbilt Lounge. Women today who think they are alone in this facility are startled to discover the presence of a ghostly entity. All at once, the perfume of another woman fills the room for a few minutes and then vanishes, leaving no trace. Other times, the ghostly perfume lingers like an aftereffect in the room, and occupants easily mistake it for the fragrance worn by a living person who has just left. The ghost's scent is patchouli, an aromatic oil. This scent is very distinctive, and though detected nowhere else in the clubhouse, it mysteriously turns up in the women's restroom. Why the ghost manifests as perfume is anyone's guess. Perhaps the scent was the last trace of the dying girl, and so it lingers through time. Perhaps, through perfume, the ghost seeks to cover up the violence that happened to her in that shadow-stricken place.

While the tale of murder lives on, the Bar Harbor Club has been subject to a number of wild stories. Though most of these accounts have no factual basis, they are disturbing in that each of them singles out the club as a place of dark forces. In fact, no other famous landmark from the town attracts so many horrifying ghost stories. In one lurid tale, the old clubhouse was the setting for the accidental death of a homeless man who broke into the club when it was closed for the winter. He was once a member of the club's elite, but had lost everything in the stock market. In one of the rooms, he turned on a light before drifting off to sleep. During the night, hypothermia set in and turned him into a frozen corpse.

The legend goes that, to this day, a light is kept on in that room —otherwise the ghost will manifest as the sounds of moans and breaking glass. This story is pure fabrication. Another tale in this category involves a young boy who drowned in the original swimming pool, which has since been filled in. Supposedly, the boy's wispy spirit wanders lost in the gardens during the early hours of the morning. Unless the accident happened at the old Bar Harbor Swimming Club, which stood on the grounds, then the story of the boy's death is untrue, for no one has ever drowned in the pool at the Bar Harbor Club. Other tales involve the spirit of a maid, an elderly woman who died far away but whose spirit returned to haunt the old site of the servants' quarters and float through the grand rooms as if she still worked there. Another alleged phantom inspires a feeling of speechless dread. People report a disturbing feeling of being watched in the Rockefeller Ballroom from an invisible presence lurking in the shadows of the stage.

Strangely, in all the lore of the Bar Harbor Club, its alleged ghosts are not the privileged founding members, but rather the poor hapless victims of age, poverty, murder, and accident. These spirits of the unfortunate seem oddly out of place in such a setting of wealth and exclusivity. One cannot help wondering why the Bar Harbor Club attracts so many ghost stories, and why these ghost stories consistently replay the death of those who are defenseless. There seems to be a deep malevolence built into the structure or working its way out of the soil. Perhaps the ghost stories from the Bar Harbor Club are best understood as masks, or ways of putting a face on what remains essentially unknown.

The earliest white settlers shunned the land where the Bar Harbor Club stands. They referred to the ground near the sandbar as the "devil's half acre," meaning that it was cursed with a certain claim to darkness. Later, bitter land disputes left their imprint on the property. In the late 1800s, Native Americans, who had been pushed off most of the island, were living in camps on the present property of the Bar Harbor Club, near the sand bar that leads out to Bar Island. Skyrocketing land values led to the eviction of these Native Americans, who were uprooted from their settlement and relocated to a tent village at the present site of the Bar Harbor Athletic Grounds, below Strawberry Hill. On the location of the former Indian settlement, a swimming club rose up at the turn of the century, and in 1929 the whole facility became the Bar Harbor Club.

The Bar Harbor Club continues to stand above the sandbar, the reach, and Bar Island. The terraced grounds and the new pool house are truly spectacular, as is the spa, but intense luxury and elaborate landscaping cannot eradicate the past history of this place in the supernatural lore of the island. Truly, the Bar Harbor Club stands out as the one landmark in the village most overshadowed by gruesome claims to the supernatural. Over and over again, these tales point to a nameless terror that still clings to this place.

The CURSE of SCHOONER HEAD

Of all the famous sights in Acadia National Park, one stands out in terms of supernatural encounters. Schooner Head is a huge outcrop of stone jutting into the Atlantic. While the land is private property, the natural formation and its stunning views are easily visible from the Schooner Head Lookout and from a park trail that goes directly down to the shore. Few who visit the spot know the history of horror hanging over Schooner Head and the land around it. A ghost ship with a terrifying wraith factors into this past, and so does a death cave ringing with the cries of the drowned. As if all these were not enough, the place also contains a fatal mansion.

The first set of ghost sightings concerns the origin of the name given to Schooner Head. One theory holds that the name comes from the way the whitish face of the rock resembles a schooner ship in full sail. The only problem is that this resemblance is by no means apparent without a huge stretch of the imagination. The other theory involves a ghost ship, a phantom schooner, as the source of the name. Supporting this claim are the recurring sightings over the centuries of a ghost ship in this precise location.

Thinking they were seeing a real sailing vessel, the British fired upon the phantom schooner during the War of 1812. The same thing happened earlier, during the presidency of Thomas Jefferson, when a federal gunboat was chasing a smugglers' craft. The smugglers disappeared into the fog in Frenchman Bay. When the ghost ship appeared, federal agents mistook it for the smugglers' boat and let loose a volley of canon fire that left its mark on the battered face of Schooner Head. Even earlier, sailors reported sightings of the phantom schooner "flitting in the moonlight off the rocks of Schooner Head," and so have rum-runners during Prohibition.

When the time and the conditions are right, anyone who is out at Schooner Head might witness the return of this ghost ship. The optimum conditions are a moonlit night with a bank of fog slowly engulfing the land. The flickering appearance of the phantom schooner is unmistakable. Silvery in the moonlight, the large four-masted vessel bears down on the huge rocks of Schooner Head, eventually crashing into the land. Before the ghost ship manifests its destruction, the atmosphere changes drastically over the area of Schooner Head. A feeling of nameless dread grows with increasing intensity. Anyone close enough will see a figure at the wheel of the vessel. This is the white woman, or the "weird helmsman" as she was reported in the *Bar Harbor Record* back in 1885. The vision of this specter has etched itself into the minds of those who have seen her. The ghost is on her knees before the wheel of the doomed ship. The dark hair of the phantom streams into the wind, and her skin is ghastly white, like a corpse from the sea.

The story of this wraith goes back to a pirate ship filled with rich stores of gold looted in the West Indies. With this fortune, the pirates came to Mount Desert Island, where they had a secret stash. On board was a dark-haired woman who supposedly doomed the ship, for back then sailors considered women and clergymen unlucky on a voyage. The woman was the wife of the pirate skipper, whose crew now numbered thirteen. Reaching Mount Desert Island, the pirates encountered heavy fog, then a British warship. Hoping to elude the warship by pulling into Otter Cove, they overshot their mark, and crashed onto the rocks of Schooner Head. When disaster struck, the skipper's wife fell to her knees and prayed for salvation. But the unforgiving rocks split the schooner apart. The angry sea dragged the pieces down into oblivion. The British sailors on the nearby warship witnessed the whole event in speechless wonder.

Close by lurk the horrors of the Anemone Cave. Unlike Schooner Head, this natural formation lies within the borders of Acadia National Park. Anyone is free to visit the site, yet officials have taken down the sign that pointed out the location of the Anemone Cave because too many people drowned there. If you go, restrict your visit to a very short window: a half hour before low tide to a half hour after low tide. All depends on the conditions of the seas, with their tendency to send surging walls of water into the coast. Too often victims of the cave have realized that they cannot escape the cold surge and fierce battering inside the granite cavern.

On certain nights, the dead can be heard talking inside the dark interior of the Anemone Cave. The experience of hearing these faint voices is unforgettable, and deeply disturbing, for the spirits all convey the utmost note of suffering and despair. Sometimes these ghosts replay their final torment by crying out and gasping for breath. Other times, the cave echoes the faraway sound of voices sobbing for the release of their souls. Most dreadful of all are the sounds of something—like a human body—being battered against the inside of the cavern by the incoming waves. Some believe that the dead hope to lure people into the cave, to exchange one life for the release of a trapped soul.

The cursed heritage of this region finds its pinnacle in a lethal mansion wrapped in a spell of darkness. This house is not the large residence of recent origin built on the very tip of Schooner

Head. Instead, the doomed mansion dates from 1912 and stands alone in the shadows of Champlain Mountain. Perched on the rocky bluffs of Frenchman Bay, the house commands a sweeping view of the Porcupine Islands, the Gouldsboro Hills, the Schoodic Peninsula, and the open ocean. The mansion, called High Seas, can be glimpsed from Schooner Head Road, but the property is not open to the public. During the Great Fire of 1947, the flames literally went around High Seas, leaving the mansion completely untouched, although the fire swept away every single other house on the road.

High Seas grew out of a doomed love affair linked to the greatest sea disaster of all time. Rudolph Brunnow, a German professor of ancient studies at Princeton University, built the house while courting Edith Evans. In their hikes out to Schooner Head, the couple found the area so captivating that Brunnow eventually purchased the twelve-acre lot. He proposed marriage, but Edith asked for some time to consider. She liked her freedom, and was not quite ready to take over Brunnow's household—he was a widower with five children. Edith then traveled to Europe while Rudolph went ahead and had the house built. The thirty-room Georgian-style mansion has no lawn, for the giant residence clings to the rocks above the roiling sea. Fred Savage designed the stately residence, built of tapestry bricks and containing a host of wonders, including a secret chamber.

Almost from the start, High Seas was enveloped in a dark cloud of tragedy. When the mansion was completed, Rudolph Brunnow sent for Edith Evans, and this time she accepted his proposal, boarding an ocean liner from Liverpool, England, to New York. Unfortunately, Edith never lived to see the mansion on the Schooner Head Road because the ship she embarked on was the *Titanic*. She drowned with more than 1,500 others on the night of April 15, 1912. Her death was famous at the time because she voluntarily gave her seat in a lifeboat to another woman who had children. Even before Edith died, people on Mount Desert Island reported seeing strange lights around High Seas, a phantom luminescence that came and went in the night. As always, the fog dragged in a nameless dread that seemed to hover over the place.

When he learned of the death of the woman he loved, Brunnow was devastated, yet a mountain slide of misfortune lay just ahead. In the fall of 1916, Brunnow's son contracted polio and died two days later. When Edward Beckwith, the boy's uncle, visited High Seas to console the grieving family, he suffered a terrible fall in a mountain-climbing accident. Six months after the death of his son, Brunnow contracted pneumonia and died inside the mansion in two days. Reporting on this, the *Bar Harbor Times* described his death as "the last in a series of tragedies that have seemed to befall the Brunnow home ever since the handsome villa was constructed nearby." The surviving family members ran for their lives, leaving the residence and never looking back.

High Seas stood empty for a few years until Eva Van Cortland Hawkes purchased the estate in 1928. Soon afterward, her only daughter died, yet Hawkes held onto the place. Despite her attachment to the mansion, something about it always frightened her, a lurking dread that would return in the night, especially when fog rolled in off Schooner Head. She eventually employed a night watchman to guard the house while she slept. It was Eva Hawkes who changed the name of the place from Meadow Brook, its original name, to High Seas. Hawkes herself died one evening inside the mansion, and it later became the property of Jackson Labs. Since then, the recurring death of hikers on the Precipice Trail directly above High Seas continues the deathly legacy of the place.

In records and accounts going back centuries, a force of evil weighs down on the landscape around Schooner Head. And the land around it casts a spell of damnation that chills the visitor to the bone. Along with the fog and the darkness, a feeling of dread always returns to claim these tormented shores.

12
HAUNTING at COMPASS HARBOR

In terms of ghostly atmosphere, nothing surpasses the Compass Harbor Nature Trail. Less than a mile from downtown Bar Harbor, the trail begins from the ocean side of Main Street. The visitor quickly enters a strange place of spellbound silence. In its eerie shores and mysterious ruins, Compass Harbor offers nothing less than a lost world haunted by the phantoms of the past.

A supernatural veil hangs over the very beginning of the trail. The forest is clearly an overgrown park from a stately mansion that once stood on these shores. The path follows the remains of a long avenue lined in places by quarried granite along the banks of a gloomy stream. The hush of the place is intense, for Compass Harbor is somehow cut off completely from the bustling world of nearby Bar Harbor. Indeed the trail soon leads the visitor into a haunted forest of exposed roots like claws. Here begins a maze of vague paths branching off into many different directions. Compass Harbor contained the first formal gardens on all of Mount Desert Island. Many of the trees here are cultivated varieties left to grow wild, enormous rhododendrons and Japanese pines. The cedar grove, in particular, stands as a ghostly trace of an intricate garden from long ago. In the center of this grove is a circle of enormous yew trees, ancient symbols of death and rebirth.

In the forest of forking paths lurks the specter of the caretaker. This disturbing phantom appears only peripherally. The image is always the same, a dark-haired man in blue. The spirit appears only for a flash, and then he's gone, returning when least expected. In this way, the ghost seems to stalk hikers on the trail. At night, the caretaker's spirit manifests as a phantom light that weaves mysteriously among the trees. Although this spirit seems threatening, he does not harm anyone, only watches obsessively over the forest and the nearby ruins.

Before reaching the sea, the trails pass the remains of a great estate that once stood over Compass Harbor. First come the remnants of the caretaker's house, located on a small, sunny knoll off to the right. These consist of the imprint of the driveway, a sunken cellar hole, and some piles of broken bricks from the chimney. Soon after the caretaker's house, in the direction of the water, come the shadowy ruins of the mansion. All that's left are the back verandas and the granite steps leading down to the beach, but these are impressive enough. The herringbone brickwork on the veranda is beautiful and leaves a haunting footprint of the vanished mansion and the famous people who once stayed there. The great staircase to the water looks like something from a lost civilization. Yet a feeling of unease hangs over the place, caused in part by the flashing surveillance of the caretaker spirit, who will come as far as the ruins, but no farther. Over the years, on a certain tree beside the veranda, a rope keeps reappearing to hang ominously or sway even when there is no breeze.

Oldfarm was the name of the shingle-style mansion that once

stood here. The Queen Anne Victorian was built in 1877, and it survived the fire of 1947 only to be demolished four years later. The house was built by the Dorr family, with fortunes that originated from the East India trade out of Salem, Massachusetts. The mansion was the setting for the supernatural from the very beginning. William James, a pioneer in the field of paranormal studies, visited the place, as did Edith Wharton, famous for her ghost stories. After the death of one of the Dorr sons, psychic mediums regularly conducted séances at Oldfarm to communicate with the dead.

The last owner of Oldfarm was George Bucknam Dorr, the father of Acadia National Park. Working with others, he made possible the protection of 35,000 acres of land into a stunning national park. Acadia National Park contains the highest elevation of land directly on the ocean along the whole eastern seaboard of the United States and Central America. As a landmark out at sea, Mount Desert Island contains an exceptionally rich history of early settlement and exploration. Without Dorr's leadership and personal sacrifices, these historic lands would not be protected for the enjoyment of future generations. He began his work in 1901, and devoted the rest of his life, health, and personal fortune to the project. He bought many tracts of land that became part of the park, and he donated acreage he already owned, including his family's Compass Harbor estate, Oldfarm, which he gave to the park in 1942.

At the end of his life, George Dorr had spent all of his enormous inheritance, and sadly, he lost his sight completely. But he had succeeded in making his dream of a national park come true. President Woodrow Wilson conferred the status of a national monument in 1916, and then in 1919, the status of a national park. Throughout the last years of his life, Dorr depended increasingly upon the assistance of his caretaker, John Rich, a man of fierce loyalty. When Dorr's money was gone, and he needed constant care, he moved into the caretaker's cottage on the grounds of the estate. Day after day, the caretaker helped Dorr along the forest paths at Compass Harbor or assisted him down the long set of stairs to the water's edge, where the man could listen to the thundering surf.

On August 5, 1944, at the age of eighty-nine, George Dorr died of heart failure on one of these walks. While his spirit has moved on, the same cannot be said of the caretaker, who haunts the forest and ruins of Compass Harbor. Everything points to John Rich as the identity of this ghost, but other possibilities exist. The land on which Oldfarm stood was once the Cousen's Farm, one of the earliest land grants on the island. Perhaps the phantom stalker belongs to a person who lived at Compass Harbor long before John Rich was born. No one will ever know the true identity of the watchman spirit. At any rate, reaching the coast, we elude this persistent phantom.

In addition to a stunning rocky outcrop called Dorr Point, the park shoreline consists of frontage on Compass Harbor, strewn with granite blocks from Dorr's old swimming pool, which the ocean filled and the sun warmed. Somewhere in this area, perhaps on the private property of nearby estates, is a very old Indian burial ground. French Jesuits passing by in the summer of 1613 reported on a funeral occurring on the shores of Compass Harbor. The spirit that returns to this place does not appear to be Native American, yet no one knows her true form. She materializes at dusk as the apparition of a young woman hurrying down the overgrown avenue, through the haunted forest, and past the ruins of Oldfarm. Her destination is the shore, and if the moon has already risen, she can be clearly seen walking down to the tip of Dorr Point and then, most strangely, disappearing into the sea.

Compass Harbor offers a walk into a phantom world of owl-ridden woods and rumbling shores. Ghosts stalk Compass Harbor, but it is the faceless spirit of the place that leaves the strongest impression. Infinitely remote from the everyday world, Compass Harbor casts its own kind of spell. It is a place that is haunting in beauty and paranormal history.

13
GHOSTS *from the* BACK SIDE

The back side is an island term referring to the western part of Mount Desert Island, a place steeped in the supernatural. Far removed from bustle and glamour of Somes Sound and Frenchman Bay, the back side remains a place of sheer natural beauty and over-powering mystery. Private coves, beaches of crushed shells, and the islands of Blue Hill Bay enchant the eye, but do not be deceived. The back side is a place crowded with the dead. An extraordinary number of ghosts stalk the back side. For some unknown reason, spirits never leave, and they sometimes gather in spectacles of horror as well as mystic wonder.

Our first stop is Spirit Cove, located off the Cape Road in Tremont. Spirit Cove is the original name for the place now called Sawyers Cove. It contains some lovely coastline, with a small beach overlooking the white sands of Merman Ledge, named for the master of a ship once wrecked there. Spirit Cove is accessible by water, not land, since the roads to the shore are private drives. This whole cove earned its name as a place that contains the souls of drowned sailors. Whenever the sea has claimed a local man or woman, people have seen a ghost ship depart from Spirit Cove to collect the soul.

The fully rigged phantom ship leaves from the eastern arm of the cove, still called Galley Point. The ghost ship sails until it finds the soul of the drowned person and then it brings that spirit back to the cove. Days later, the ghost appears alone on the shoreline or grouped with other phantoms among the dark spruce trees on the western end of the cove, known as Stewart Head. One wonders if these spirits have any choice in their passage to this place and their confinement here through the centuries.

Moving on, we pass the swamp graves. Anyone who has traveled through the back side cannot help noticing the remarkable number of graveyards, cemeteries, and family burial plots that dot the landscape. What many do not know is that the back side is filled with many more unmarked graves, some dating back to ancient Native American settlements. There is one such place of unmarked graves that stands out from the rest in terms of burial practices and paranormal encounters.

The location is Murphy Swamp, in Seal Cove. Here, around the perimeter of the marsh, are a number of unmarked burial sites. It was very unusual for Native Americans to bury their dead in low, wet ground, and the practice suggests a time of crisis, like plague or warfare, in which a large number of people needed quick burials. Other possibilities point to the burial of people who were shunned, outcasts of the community, or victims of murder. Whatever the case in Seal Cove, the unmarked graves in Murphy Swamp tell a disturbing tale.

On the Kellytown Road, already infamous for the brutal murder of a man found stuffed into a well, some of the homes and byways suffer disturbances by the ancient spirits from the swamp graves. When Kelly Carter lived out there, she had an experience she will never forget. One night as she was getting out of the shower, she wiped two large mirrors to see herself. When she cleaned the mist from the mirrors, she clearly saw an Indian woman walking through her bathroom. Kelly spun around, but no one was there. After some research, she learned that the area around her house was a burial site for Native Americans who once lived on that side of the island. Other spirits from Murphy Swamp appear as shadowy figures standing frozen over unmarked gravesites or staggering through the alder trees. As in the case of Kelly Carter, these ghosts manifest best in mirrors. Characteristically, motorists look into their rear-view mirrors and witness these fleeting shades of darkness.

A couple miles south, the spirit of another Native American woman haunts the shores of West Tremont. Tinker Brook is a small creek that swells with the tide on Goose Cove. The spirit here returns late at night, first as the sound of paddling on the water when the tide is high. Nearby residents have gone outside, intrigued by the sound, and the sight that follows is always the same. Silvery in the moonlight, the apparition of a Native American woman in a birch-bark canoe slowly paddles down Tinker Creek to Goose Cove. She gradually disappears, gliding in the direction of Blue Hill Bay. Not surprisingly, the apparition follows an ancient migratory route once used by Native Americans on these shores. Through the dews of summer and the gales of winter, the ghost sets out in her canoe, over and over again, suggesting that this wraith is doomed forever to repeat a journey never completed.

Our next stop is Spook Hill, in West Tremont, where the land rises to its highest prominence. A weird static energy hangs over the place, and if lightning strikes, it will always hit Spook Hill. Spirits of the back side seem particularly concentrated here. Some of these are creepy guardian spirits, ghosts of deceased people who appear to look over and care for the young children of the neighborhood. Coming home from school one day in winter, a young boy was accidentally sent to his babysitter when no one was home, and the house was locked. Yet the ghost of an old man appeared, shadowy through the curtains, to unlatch the front door very slowly. When the confused boy entered the house, he could not see the man, but the boy heard something shuffling around in the kitchen. A spell-like atmosphere inside the house quickly overtook the child and, tossing his winter jacket onto a chair, he went immediately upstairs and fell into a deep sleep. When his babysitter returned, she found the boy alone in the locked house, his jacket neatly hung on a hook far too high for the boy to reach. A similar event occurred in a nearby house. A child awoke one night to see the apparition of an old Victorian woman in black leaning over the bed and pulling up the covers.

At the very crest of the hill stands a haunted farmhouse from the 1840s. This is the Lawson house on its fifteen-acre lot. Although the place has been empty for years, you won't find anyone trespassing here because people know enough to stay away from this haunted house. The curtains open and close by themselves, and sometimes a lit candle glows in an upstairs window. Night after night the ghost of an old man returns to sit and smoke a pipe on the front porch. The smell of tobacco sometimes lingers on the lawn. Woe be it to anyone who disturbs the peace of this watchful spirit! Perhaps no one knows the place better than Linda Graham, who has lived across the street since 1974. She has seen the apparition on countless occasions, and has spoken with many other witnesses, including a state trooper who stopped to ask if anyone lived in the Lawson house because he swore that he had seen an old man smoking on the front porch. Perry Lawson once lived in the house, and he guarded it so possessively that he still inhabits the place as a watchful spirit. One time, the ghost even drove off the tax assessor, who had been given keys to the house. Old Man Lawson slammed doors repeatedly inside the house until the terrified assessor beat a hasty retreat.

Most fascinating of all are the phantom pirates from Spook Hill who form processions through the night. Appearing as completely black shapes of men, these ghosts walk in single file, and they hold glowing lanterns that cast no shadows and shed no light on their surroundings. Each time this strange procession takes place, the dark apparitions follow a long-unused shore road that runs from Goose Cove to the top of Spook Hill. Although this road has grown over with trees and bushes, the procession follows the original path with unerring accuracy. Many of these coves have a history of smuggling, and in the lore of the region, the dark phantoms are the spirits of dead pirates who buried treasure somewhere on Spook Hill. Long before the procession reaches the crest of the hill, ghostly manifestations will have taken place on Goose Cove. Especially on foggy nights, people report strange lights on the water coming to shore.

For whatever reason, ghosts congregate on the back side, in the form of phantom processions on Goose Cove, recurring apparitions in Murphy Swamp, and crowds of drowned mariners out on Spirit Cove. The dead still inhabit their old houses and even manifest themselves to care for the local children. For centuries, a Native American wraith has tried unsuccessfully to leave these shores. The strange thing about this whole place is that the dead don't move on. Some unknown force keeps the spirits bound to the back side.

14
WRECK *of the*
GRAND DESIGN

S hip Harbor, located at the southern end of Mount Desert Island, is a haunting locale for tales of otherworldly terror. On the surface, nothing could be more picturesque than the pink granite cliffs and the green wooded shoreline of spruce and tamarack. Visitors walk the Ship Harbor Nature Trail for a mile and a half along the cove. Despite its natural beauties, Ship Harbor exudes an oppressive air of gloom and fear, a symptom of its tortured past. Truly, the place has a hidden side. It is a land of sudden fog, unsolved mysteries, and hungry spirits.

The wreck of the *Grand Design* is the source of the supernatural legends in the area. In 1739 autumn gales drove the three-ton wooden vessel drastically off course, and it ran aground on Long Ledge, at the entrance to the Western Way. The entire ship's company escaped in boats and landed in the nearby cove now known as Ship Harbor.

The salvation of the crew and passengers was short-lasting, and many later wished they had perished beneath the waves. Two hundred people were aboard the ill-fated vessel. Most were passengers from Northern Ireland bound for a new life in Pennsylvania. On the shores of Ship Harbor, the company built temporary shelters, creating a base from which to explore the island and find assistance. Little did they dream of the darkness that lay in store for them.

Even before all the deaths and disappearances, something strange and awful seemed to be at hand. To begin with, *no one* was living on the island. After escaping from the shipwreck, the people searched the entire island, which they found completely uninhabited. In vain, crews rowed around the island in skiffs, calling out and looking for people or signs of habitation. They found nothing whatsoever. A deathly quiet hung over the bays and inlets, suggesting that a great and menacing power lay constantly in wait. The French were gone, and so too the English. The Wabanaki Indians, who traditionally migrated to the island in the fall, were nowhere to be seen, and their overgrown villages were long since abandoned.

The tragic and baffling fate of the *Grand Design*'s passengers shapes the ghost stories from Ship Harbor. The enormous mortality certainly figures into some of the tales told—as many as ninety-four unmarked graves in the woods along the eastern shoreline lend themselves to supernatural encounters. Marooned for months in the silent cove as winter set in, the company salvaged supplies from the grounded ship and fished and hunted, but still a slow starvation set in. Exposure and death kept reducing the ranks of the survivors. Dead bodies were laid in hastily assembled, rock grave mounds.

The souls of some of those buried at Ship Harbor remain trapped in the cove where they died waiting for salvation. Some people report being strangely depleted of energy in certain spots at Ship Harbor, as if the dead buried nearby took their pangs of starvation to their graves—along with the desperation to feed. Most of the spirits here are weak, semi-transparent impressions from another world, most often perceived as an atmosphere of gloom. More than one hiker on the Ship Harbor Nature Trail has been struck by the feeling of a sad or plaintive presence, or even a peripheral glimpse of an emaciated man composed only of light and shadow. One must pay careful attention in order to observe these faint spirits. Ghostly encounters at the place are easily mistaken for a cold gust from the sea, the wailing cry of a herring gull, or a sudden feeling of faintness. One thing is certain—Ship Harbor is a *heavy* place.

The greatest legend of Ship Harbor concerns the fate of the search party sent out by the passengers of the *Grand Design*. When the survivors determined that the island was uninhabited, they formed a search party to cross the island and reach the mainland to the north. As stated in the earliest account, "Making the best shift for shelter and subsistence which their situation would permit, they dispatched a party of one hundred of their most able and vigorous young men to the mainland, in hopes of finding a settlement there from whom assistance might be obtained."

The formation of the search party reveals not just the hopes of the survivors, but also their fears. Clearly, the people were in a general state of panic and alarm, for why else would they send out so many armed men when a much smaller dispatch would have sufficed? Dividing up their rations and supplies, the people gave half of all they had to the strongest in their group. What the survivors did was establish a search party in the form of a militia. In late October or early November, these young men marched off bravely into the dark interior of the terror-infested island.

The search party apparently never reached the mainland—in fact they were never seen or heard of again. The entire search party of one hundred men disappeared, leaving no trace whatsoever. In the words of the historical record, "Nothing further was ever seen or heard of this part of their companions." The loss of the search party remains a mystery comparable to the vanishing of one hundred and eighteen settlers in Roanoke, Virginia, in 1589.

In the whispered lore of Down East Maine, a dark force, bound to the island, was unleashed during this time period. The indigenous peoples have inhabited Mount Desert Island for more than five thousand years, yet they abruptly left the place around 1700 and stayed away for more than half a century. Indeed, the Indians shunned the island, as if fleeing the advance of something unspeakably menacing. The wreck of the *Grand Design* took place during those "black years"—a nearly complete gap in the historical record of the place. It was a time shrouded in secrecy—and a time when the island earned its reputation as a dreaded place.

Certainly, death and danger hung over the area during the French and Indian Wars, while smallpox and other diseases swept their deadly course. Yet there was something more to the horror instilled by the island. A force of darkness now walked the land. Native American lore from the region is replete with dangerous supernatural forces—the place contained much "bad medicine." Malicious spirits, demons, even cannibalistic entities belonged to the landscape of Acadia. In addition to the *wendigo*, an Indian devil, most dreaded of all was the *cheenoo*, a murderous ghost that came down from the deep north.

Though terribly late, assistance eventually came to the survivors of the shipwreck back at Ship Harbor. A passing party of Native Americans, noticing the tattered red clothes and bed sheets tied to trees, came to the people's assistance, carrying letters to settlers in Warren, Maine. When finally rescued during the gales of winter, only six people survived out of the two hundred passengers who landed safely in Ship Harbor. Since then, the cove has been something of a cursed site, a source of frequent shipwrecks, though none as devastating as that of 1739.

Sad and heart wrenching, the wreck of the *Grand Design* is also deeply disturbing. In the cove of lost souls doomed to wait for eternity, encounters with the dead occur on a daily basis. Yet in the baffling fate of the lost search party stands a deeper source of supernatural horror. The ghost tales of Ship's Harbor and the *Grand*

Design hint at regions of stark terror, the bleak shores of the complete unknown, and—worst of all—a glimpse into the dark heart of the island.

15
The GATES to HELL

The Devil's Oven is the most infamous gateway to the supernatural on Mount Desert Island. The sea cave, with its long dramatic approach along a tortured coastline, has been the setting of ghostly encounters going back thousands of years. The striking thing about these accounts is the unmistakable evil they foretell, and the dark rituals of horror they recount. Indeed, the place is dangerous ground. One must approach the Devil's Oven with caution, if not some form of spiritual protection, for this section of Hull's Cove is more aptly called Hell's Cove.

A beach cave of large proportions, the Devil's Oven presents ten-foot ceilings and a deep, gloomy interior. From inside, it offers some stunning views of blue water framed by the dark maw of the cavern. From the outside, the cave looks almost like the two eye sockets of a skull, for a rocky ledge divides the enclosure into two chambers. Commonly known as the Ovens, the cave earned its original name from Native Americans living in the area long before English settlement. The cavern, located between Hull's Cove and Salisbury Cove, is not easily accessible. If you are going by foot, it is best to start out from the beach near DeGregoire Park, less than a mile away. Head north, or left, when you first get to the shore, and restrict your exploration to the cave itself, for the land around it is private property. Most importantly, be sure to consult a tide chart before starting out, for the cave is under water much of the time.

Like scenes from a blasted inferno, the coastal approach to the Devil's Oven tells a tale in itself. The place resembles a landscape from the underworld. Deposits of sulfur and iron give a fiery look to the blasted cliffs that rise up from the shore. In other places, especially where water seeps down, the rocks appear pitch black. It is apparent that the land has never healed. The coastline looks as if it was formed only yesterday, not millions of years ago. The rocks form sharp jagged peaks totally unlike the worn granite shoreline characteristic of Acadia.

Close to the Devil's Oven an atmosphere of insidious evil permeates the haunted coastline. Here, in places all along the base of the cliffs, the waves have pecked out little "ovens," or demon caves. Then, as though signifying a depraved church devoted to the forces of darkness, a huge detached wall of cliff called the Cathedral juts into the water. In this giant rock is an opening called the *Via Mala,* a corrupted Latin term for the Evil Way or Road to Evil. Of course, the gateway leads right to the Devil's Oven, like an enormous half-buried skull, with baleful eyes glaring out of twenty-foot cliffs.

The Devil's Oven has been the setting of strange encounters for time immemorial. Native Americans reported seeing strange lights out there, like glowing orbs or great fires burning inside the cavern, regardless of whether or not the place was under water. In fact, Native Americans considered the whole cliff face on the north side of the island to be evil ground, and they shunned the area. If circumstances required them to go there, they wore charms and took other protective measures. They believed the rocks contained portals or entryways to hell, and the Devil's Oven was the main gateway. Long before contact with Christian missionaries, local Indians had their own concept of hell as a place of darkness inhabited by terrifying entities and tormented souls.

Strange sights and sounds are still reported in and around the Devil's Oven. Accounts from the 1880s testify to "a weird, lurid light that might be seen gleaming and flashing out from under the cliffs towards Frenchman Bay" in the area of the Devil's Oven. Also inexplicable are the sounds people have heard there—the cries of tormented souls and strange words and chants spoken in aberrant tongues. Fishermen today report mysterious lights burning inside the sea cavern. For centuries the belief has persisted that danger befalls anyone who sees the phantom fires.

The Devil's Oven earns its name from the cavern's ancient purpose. The setting of dark rites, the sea cave was where people died agonizing deaths by being burned alive inside a literal oven. Outrageous as it sounds, the practice of roasting people in the Devil's Oven is a documented fact passed down in the historical records of the region. The gruesome practice was reserved for people viewed as especially evil or dangerous. More feared than a torturous death inside the Devil's Oven was the danger of damnation, for the oven could reputedly devour a soul, pulling it literally into hell. It's almost as if the spirits of the damned are impressed into the dark, convoluted rock of the cave. Centuries later the smoke and soot reappear over and over again to stain the cavern's roof. With ghastly endurance, the fires return to burn again as reported in stories, lore, and first-hand accounts.

No one will ever know the true number of people burned alive in the Devil's Oven. Most likely these terrible rituals took place very rarely over the centuries, and with great solemnity. Just as the incoming tide has long since washed away the ashes, many accounts are now lost, or perhaps conveniently forgotten. But in one instance, an eye-witness account has survived. It took place in the eighteenth century, and concerns a hunter and trapper named Esek Winslow.

The Micmac Indians hated Esek Winslow justifiably, for he was a notorious mercenary, hunting Native Americans for bounty during the French and Indian Wars. During one of his trips into the area, Esek Winslow encountered a group of Micmacs, who captured him and killed the group of mercenaries under his command. To the dreaded sea cavern went Winslow, bound and gagged, and there his captors lashed him with rawhide to a wooden stake driven deep into the pebble beach inside the cavern. A pile of sticks and brush was heaped around the stake and at last was set on fire. The man would be consumed in body by the fire—and in soul by the devil of the place.

Meanwhile, as night fell across the land, the Native Americans grew increasingly uneasy. Even with protective paint and talismans, they avoided the place completely after sundown. Since the wood piled around the stake was green and damp, the fire burned slowly, although it created a lot of smoke. Finally, the Micmacs left their enemy staked in a smoldering cloud, figuring that he would die by drowning, if not by fire, for the tide had turned and was now coming in. Casting off hurriedly in canoes through the deepening twilight, they left Esek Winslow to his allotted doom. Amazingly, Esek survived his ordeal, for the fire took so long to catch that the rising tide put it out. The cavern filled slowly with water, until the cold salty waves reached his chin. The buoyancy of the water and his constant struggling loosened the stake, enabling Winslow to escape.

Ghastly accounts in the history of Mount Desert testify to traditions of horror at the Devil's Oven. Without a doubt, these atrocities contribute to the supernatural sightings that still plague the place. This is not surprising, since the cavern forms a gateway to realms of the infernal. Through this doorway travel the phantoms of people who committed murder in the cave or died there. In attendance are demon spirits, if not the devil himself.

When this happens, the tide-bound cavern will echo in howling cries and the sound of strange, mystic incantations. Then, as always, the fires will burn again, whether or not the cave is under water. These are the phantom fires. Should they start up, then you must pray for a speedy deliverance. Do not even look back in your frantic scramble to leave this cursed place.

16
The PROVING GROUND

Winter Harbor, Maine, is the setting for this dark tale of ghostly encounters that go back generations. The village, only four miles by water from Bar Harbor, seems like a world apart. A wild and eerie quality haunts the landscape and is reflected in the extremities of the entire Schoodic Peninsula—towering cliffs and forty-foot sprays of seawater. On these rugged shores lies a secret source of supernatural power inextricably tied to the land. People live in constant fear because this ancient terror refuses to go away.

In the center of the village, overlooking Frenchman Bay, the land rises to a point known by the earliest settlers as Bow-Arrow Hill. For as long as anyone can remember, this particular spot has been the setting of extreme psychic encounters. Strange orbs, accompanied by a whirring sound, appear in the area all the time, and almost everyone in Winter Harbor has seen weird lights in the skies. The old houses built on Bow-Arrow Hill are susceptible to sudden and deafening banging and rattling, and sometimes these unaccountable noises come from within the walls of the houses. It is not uncommon for residents to jump up in terror in the middle of the night because their beds are shaking violently. Only a short time ago, a young woman was talking on the phone when she saw a potted plant in her house suddenly burst into flames.

Perhaps no one knows these occurrences better than members of the Bickford and Whitney families, who have lived there for generations. For them, a shocking ghostly manifestation is simply a part of everyday life. Their experiences shed light on the secrets of Bow-Arrow Hill and the mysterious force gathered there, for these accounts include glimpses into a central figure, a spiritual combatant or dark warrior.

This evil spirit has reappeared over the years in an uncanny fashion. Betty Williams saw the phantom in the 1950s, when she lived at the Bickford House, at the crest of the hill. She was thirteen and had gone to the store to buy cigarettes for her father. When she returned, dusk had almost settled into night, but she could still see the shapes and outlines of her surroundings. Standing behind her father's car, she saw the black silhouette of a man. She approached the figure, thinking it was her father. The black phantom turned and headed toward the attached barn of the house. Betty followed, calling out, "Dad? Dad?" The dark figure never stopped or turned around. Instead, he nearly led Betty into the pitch-black barn. On the threshold she felt a sudden shudder of cold revulsion and realized something was terribly wrong. She turned around and ran back to the house, where she found her father. They searched the barn, but the black figure had vanished.

Linda Whitney, who grew up in the Bickford House, had her own unforgettable encounter with the ominous specter. This happened in the 1960s, when she was thirteen. Lying in bed one night she heard loud footsteps overhead in the attic. The footsteps came down the stairs, and to her horror she then beheld the phantom in her room. The figure appeared solid, the shape of a man composed entirely of darkness. Walking across her room, the ghost brushed by her bed but didn't stop. The phantom seemed intent on looking out the window, and Linda even saw the curtains move when the ghost pulled them aside. The figure stood there for a few minutes, looking out on Bow-Arrow Hill, while the girl shook in terror lest the phantom turn around and see her. Gradually, the ghost grew transparent and then faded away.

In 2002, when he was thirteen years old, Alex Whitney had a most chilling look at the dark figure of Bow-Arrow Hill. Alex was in bed in his room at the Whitney House, which stands a couple hundred feet from the Bickford House. Very early in the morning, before the sun had risen, the young man woke up to the sound of a horse cantering down the street between the houses. It was summer, and his window was open. Strangely, the horse followed the road past the end of the avenue, only to turn around and gallop back the way it had come. At first Alex thought his neighbor's horse had escaped its pasture and had wandered into the village. Trying to go back to sleep, he lay there, listening to the horse go back and forth, and then he remembered that his neighbor had recently moved away, taking her horse with her. Just then he heard, very clearly, the sound of the horse outside rearing up and whinnying.

Thinking the whole situation odd, Alex got up and went to his window, but he saw no horse. Something did catch his eye, however, in the upstairs bay window of the Bickford House across the way. What the boy saw was the dark figure of a man walking back and forth in front of the window. Strangely, the figure stopped and picked up a black sphere and flung it through the wall of the house. The sphere seemed weightless, yet dropped to the ground. After throwing out another sphere as well as a heavy box, the dark figure walked away from the window. Moments later, Alex saw the ghost step through the second-floor wall of the house and proceed to walk down a staircase that did not exist. Transfixed, his heart pounding, Alex watched the dark figure abruptly stop when he reached the ground. Turning slowly, the ghost looked directly up at Alex.

The phantom's gaze conveyed a feeling of evil so strong that Alex fled to a guest bedroom on the other side of the house, but the dark specter soon followed him. His heart still pounding, Alex tried to settle his nerves by reading a book. Just as he got started, a fierce windstorm swept down outside and began howling around the vicinity of Bow-Arrow Hill. Then Alex heard footsteps coming down the hall outside his door. Through a gap at the bottom, he saw the shadow of someone walk past the door. Something about the gait led him to believe that this was not a living human being. Alex did not have to rouse the house for his defense, for the deafening sounds of pounding and banging throughout the entire structure summoned the whole household.

Surprising discoveries soon followed. Alex was so insistent on the details of his story that members of his family went to the local historical society and dug up old pictures of the Bickford House. One photo from the time the house was built in 1891 shows a door in the spot where Alex saw the figure step through the wall of the house. For more than sixty years this door has been completely hidden—plastered over inside and covered by shingles on the outside. Old Indian trails behind Bow-Arrow Hill also lend support to Alex's memory of the horse running to a point beyond the end of the road. A trail once led from the bay directly up to fields now blocked by the houses on Main Street. As testified by stone artifacts and shell heaps, Native Americans have occupied the land around Winter Harbor for thousands of years. This heritage has even informed the meaning of the name of Bow-Arrow Hill. In the oral history of the region, this particular place was once an Indian proving ground, a place of sporting events and ancient competitions.

With its history of paranormal encounters, Bow-Arrow Hill was more likely a proving ground of a spiritual nature. In other words, the place was one of combat and competition against supernatural entities. Prehistoric Native American culture provided a central place to the tribal shaman—called a *medeulin*. These men and women dealt with the spirit world on a daily basis in order to provide healing, protection, and resources for their people. A central task of a shaman was performing—actually, proving—his or her mastery over dangerous supernatural elements, and what better place to do this than Bow-Arrow Hill, a site of fearful forces? Of interest is the fact that the dark specter typically appears to people who are thirteen years of age, the time when individuals go through a rite of passage into adulthood, and the age at which shamans had to prove their powers of spiritual defense.

Sometimes the secret lies right in the name of a place. Although Bow-Arrow Hill seems to refer to a bow *and* arrow, the name might be describing a *bowed arrow*. A bowed arrow symbolizes one that can fly or swerve into another world—a different dimension—in order to track and kill its foe. Shamans from Acadia once used the bow and arrow in intricate ceremonies of exorcism. Such encounters probably took place right on Bow-Arrow Hill, still plagued with intense outbreaks of the paranormal. At the center of this psychic whirlwind is the recurrence of the dark figure, a spiritual opponent, a wraith that persists in causing speechless terror.

17
A FACE in the WATER

Seeing a ghost under water has to be one of the most unique—and terrifying—encounters. Yet this is exactly what happened in legend-haunted Bucksport, Maine. Long known to be a portal to other dimensions, the area contains vast tracts of dark wooded shores and a huge convergence of waters swirling through the Eastern Channel into the Atlantic Ocean. Bucksport is home to many spirits of the damned, but one apparition stands out in particular—the ghost seen under water. Whether it is the spirit of a woman brutally murdered, a demon, or some other supernatural entity, no one knows for sure. What remains certain is a sinister pattern of sightings. And what remains most dreadful is the face of the specter when it suddenly turns itself around.

One encounter with this water spirit happened to a young woman in the summer of 2006, when she was scuba diving in Silver Lake. Amanda and her boyfriend had gone diving on one of those perfect summer days, with the sun sparkling off the water and a light salty breeze from the southeast. The couple swam together for a while before each went off alone to explore the underwater wonders nearby. It was on one of those short forays that Amanda met the apparition. Before she saw the ghost, she heard it—gargled moans, cries, and vast bubbles of air reverberating under the water.

Amanda spun around and saw a figure a short distance away. The back was turned, but it was clearly a woman with long hair and a long dress. The woman was struggling for help, crying out in the water. Then the woman started to slump over. Amanda had no idea she was seeing a ghost. Her response was for a living, breathing person, a woman who was drowning and who could not rise from the bottom of the lake. Amanda approached the figure and even reached out to offer help. And that was when the young diver realized, with an unforgettable shock, that she was looking at a ghost.

Amanda's story parallels other sightings in the area. Two Bucksport residents, Cheryl Leach and her seventeen-year-old daughter, began having a series of disturbing dreams in the 1980s. The dreams were always the same—a woman with long hair and a long dress struggling for her life under water. For a time, the mother and daughter did not realize they were having the same dream. When they realized what was going on, they launched an investigation with author Carol Schulte and concluded that the ghost was the spirit of a murdered woman named Sarah Ware.

Sparking one of the most sensational murder trials in Maine, the brutal death of Sarah Ware riveted the world in September 1898. She was fifty-two years old, and had come from Nova Scotia, but she was working as a domestic in Bucksport at the time of her death. Most accounts of the murder place Sarah Ware at a poker game on the night she was murdered. At this gathering were many prominent men in the town—two lawyers, a city councilman, and a store owner. Rumor has it that one of the men struck her when she rejected his advances. The blow proved to be fatal, crushing her skull and killing her instantly. Other theories propose that Sarah was killed for the money she might have carried that fateful night. On one thing most accounts agree—the murder trial involved an elaborate cover-up by men of influence, and the case remains unsolved to this day.

The travesty of justice entailed one of the most notorious desecrations of the dead. Officials discovered the body of Sarah Ware in a field three weeks after her disappearance. Animals had eaten off most of her face, and her jaw and cheekbone were missing. Yet the scalp, with its long hair, remained intact. Carefully folded up under her head was Sarah's blood-stained cape. The arms of the corpse were also crossed in traditional fashion. When officials tried to pick up the body, the head fell completely off. The courts retained the skull in an evidence box. Meanwhile, city workers buried the headless body of Sarah Ware in a nearby pauper's cemetery. Eighty years after the murder, the skull, with its ghastly head of hair, turned up in the dusty courthouse. Later, with much publicity, a group of women, including a journalist and local historians, saw to it that the head receive proper burial at the site of Sarah Ware's grave.

The story doesn't end here, for Sarah's remains apparently do not lie in the grave that now contains her battered skull. For the original resting place of Sarah Ware—the pauper's cemetery used back in 1898—is now under a vast expanse of water called Silver Lake. When the town of Bucksport flooded the valley for a reservoir in the 1930s, the bodies in the pauper's cemetery supposedly received proper burial in a new graveyard. Many people suspected that some of the corpses, like that of Sarah Ware, remained in their original resting place, with only the tombstones moved for the sake of appearances. All of this points back to the motivation of the spirit. Tormented and trapped by the separation of her body, the spirit of Sarah Ware cries out, particularly to women, hoping to bring about justice in her case.

Returning to Amanda's close encounter with the wraith in the waters of Silver Lake, this theory holds, but other stark possibilities exist, all depending on how one interprets the dreadful face that Amanda beheld. For when the apparition finally turned around, it had no face. Like snakes uncoiling, the ghost's long hair floated back into the waters of the lake, revealing nothing in the place of the face—no eyes, nose, mouth, or ears. It was not a skull that Amanda saw beneath the hair, but rather the appearance of a smooth blank expanse of skin, oval in shape, where the face should have been. Gasping with horror, Amanda pulled back, wrenched herself around, and shot up to the surface. Before she reached the top, she mustered the courage to look back down. But by then the strange specter had vanished.

Several aspects of the sightings by Amanda and others, such as Cheryl Leach and her daughter, suggest that the water spirit is the ghost of Sarah Ware. The apparition of a woman with long hair and a long dress certainly resembles the historical woman, and the struggle for help under the water suggests a spirit whose body now lies at the bottom of a lake. From this perspective, the faceless quality of the ghost seen by Amanda represents the *effacement* of the corpse of Sarah Ware—headless, the skull disfigured and buried elsewhere.

By this point in our tale, the water spirit of Bucksport has earned its place in the dark canons of supernatural lore. But there is a final twist in this whole affair. Troubling parallels with other ghost accounts suggest an entity more mysterious and dreadful than the spirit of Sarah Ware. From the well-documented lore of ghosts from Asia comes an apparition that bears a striking resemblance to the entity witnessed by Amanda. For example, Japanese accounts testify to a phantom that appears as a woman sobbing and crying out for help, but concealing her face by turning away or covering it up with her hands or her long hair. When someone finally comes to the rescue, the woman reveals herself to be a ghost that has no face.

Native Americans living in the area of Bucksport, Maine, have recorded many mysterious encounters with the supernatural. Some of these involve lake monsters, water spirits, and other entities that are not of human origin, beings that possess great power to change shape and do harm. Accounts exist of a shapeshifting water spirit known as the *chipitchkam*, who persists in causing speechless dread.

For all we know, these ancient stories contain some of the first accounts of the baffling specter that still haunts the byways of Bucksport and the dreams of its residents.

18
The RETURN of HATE EVIL

The most remote and mysterious section of the Atlantic Seaboard lies east of Mount Desert Island. There is little room for commercial tourism in this land of secrets. A deep, heavy silence hangs over the blueberry barrens, the vast tracts of forest, and the isolated villages separated by a maze of inlets and salt marshes. From the heart of this twilight territory comes a truly unique and sinister ghost story. Spirits of the dead inhabit an eighteenth century inn that is still open to the public—the Chandler River Lodge in Jonesboro, Maine. Most prominent among these ghosts is the spirit of a man named Hate Evil.

Hate Evil Hall was born in 1772. Amazingly, he was the seventh generation of men in his family named Hate Evil. He was also the last man to bare the burden of this appalling name. The first Hate Evil Hall came from England in 1632 during the migration of Puritans whose fanaticism led to the Salem Witch Trials. The name of Hate Evil was supposed to mean one who despises wrongdoings. Yet the given name has the opposite effect—denoting a person embodying the darkest traits of humanity. Certainly, the last Hate Evil Hall carried his name like an affliction, for darkness always followed him. When Hate Evil Hall was a young man of twenty-five, he purchased a large tract of land overlooking the Chandler River in Jonesboro. Hate Evil built the Chandler River Lodge in 1797, and he died there in 1829. On a moss-eaten gravestone in the Village Burying Ground, his terrible name is carved for posterity.

Since his death, Hate Evil Hall has refused to leave the house he built. After more than two hundred years, the Chandler River Lodge still stands on a knoll of pines and firs surrounded by fields sloping down to the tidal river. Generations of the Hall family lived on the saltwater farm that functioned as a stagecoach inn. Although renovations were made over the years, which included raising the roof and making additions, the structure still maintains the simplicity of its plain New England style. After staying in the family for 160 years, the house became the property of the Kerr family, who continued to run the inn. The tradition continued into 2006, when the property was sold to its current owners, who made extensive improvements and reopened the place for year-round lodging and fine dining.

The phantom of Hate Evil favors the library, where he manifests as the same cloud of darkness that surrounded the man during his lifetime. Despite its lovely river views and cozy fireplace, the library contains a disturbing atmosphere of dread and gloom. This presence in the library is concentrated in a tiny adjoining study, where Hate Evil would have kept his accounts. People sometimes report a suffocating feeling of darkness in there. During the summer of 2007, a guest who enjoyed dinner in the library left behind a simple black cardigan sweater on the back of her chair. She telephoned the inn that evening and asked the staff to find her missing sweater, but it was nowhere to be found. She even stopped by the inn the next day and looked unsuccessfully before leaving town. Then, approximately two months later, the black cardigan reappeared unexpectedly on the back of the very same chair. Apparently, the spirit of Hate Evil took the sweater, drawn to its black color, like the garb of a Puritan. Although this sweater would be small on a man today, the garment would perfectly fit a male from the eighteenth century.

Hate Evil also haunts the other rooms and corridors of the lodge. Most active when the place is quiet and nearly empty, the spirit has startled more than one person in the dead of the night. A couple years ago, one woman spent an unforgettable evening as the only guest in the inn. She was staying in the Judah Chandler room on the second floor when heavy footsteps ascending the staircase woke her up. After calling out, she received no answer, and when she got up to investigate, she encountered no one. Intense stillness and deep shadows cloaked the building. Returning to bed, the uneasy guest listened for the footsteps, which never recurred. Tossing and turning, she eventually fell into a fitful sleep, only to wake up in dread as she felt a presence in the room circling around the bed. A psychic medium who visited the inn picked up on a ghostly presence hovering in one of the stairwells where the ghostly footsteps have a habit of treading in the middle of the night. Another guest may have actually seen the apparition of Hate Evil in 2010. This person arrived at the inn before the restaurant opened for dinner, so he walked around the building, and that's when he saw the ghost looking out a window. The apparition appeared as an extremely pale, middle-aged man with jet-black hair.

Other ghosts find a home in the Chandler River Inn. Undoubtedly, in a house of this age, many people died within its walls over the years, but some deaths have contributed to the ghostly history of the old place. The most recent was in 2005, when a man living alone in the inn died of a heart attack sometime during the winter. When someone finally discovered the body, it was frozen solid because the furnace had shut off. For weeks, the corpse lay in what was once a small downstairs bedroom. That room now contains a gloomy atmosphere and an icy-cold draft. George Marston was the last descendant of the Hall family to own the Chandler River Lodge. He died on August 11, 1961, of a heart attack on the cellar stairs. People working at the inn today commonly experience a nameless fright exactly where he died. While the fieldstone basement is certainly creepy enough to inspire fear, the feeling of fright only occurs when someone is leaving the cellar and heading up the stairs, just as George Marston was doing at the moment of his death.

Another spirit that roams the halls is the ghost of Sabrina Watts, who came to the inn as a young bride of twenty-one and spent the next eighty years of her life there. She was married to Horace Hall, the son of Hate Evil. Perhaps owing to the long time she spent there, Sabrina Watts refuses to leave. Sometimes, this phantom appears to assert her sovereignty over the kitchen as her own particular sphere. The ghost has the kitchen to herself during the wee hours of the night, but she must share these quarters with the chef and staff from the restaurant at other times. One evening, this ghost apparently lost her patience and caused a disturbance, clearing the room. No one was near a serving station in the hall outside the kitchen when a silver teapot shot through the air and hit the floor with a single thud, never rolling on the hard, smooth surface. Another time, an antique enamel pie pan appeared out of nowhere. Clearly well used, the pan was certainly a favorite of a cook from long ago. When workers opened the kitchen one morning, they found the old pan, which may have once belonged to Sabrina Watts. One guest caught a glimpse of this phantom and ran from the inn, vowing never to return. In the kitchen, standing near the sink, he saw the phantom figure of a woman.

The past lives on at the Chandler River Lodge, an eighteenth century inn located in the misty wilds of coastal Maine. The house built by Hate Evil Hall still stands today as a testimony to the supernatural presence that shrouds the mysterious Down East region. Fearful indeed are spirits of the dead that persist throughout the centuries, but most sinister perhaps is the return of Hate Evil. Accompanied by the darkness that always surrounded him, this specter still bears a name that conjures up our deepest fears.

19
BLUE WILLOW

F rom the Black's Woods comes a chilling tale. Located between Franklin and Cherryfield, this region lives up to its reputation as a place shrouded in supernatural legend. Going back hundreds of years, ghostly encounters have plagued this beautiful stretch of woods, lakes, and mountain crags. This story takes place in the oldest house in the area, an ancient structure dating back to 1764. Manifestations of the paranormal in this house stem from a history of tragedy and madness. Strangest of all, it is a haunted object that triggers the alarming series of events.

When Roy Montana purchased the house in 2004, he had no knowledge of its haunted reputation, but immediately after he moved into the building, the disturbances began. They consisted of loud whispering, as if from many people talking all night long at one end of the attic. Roy went up there on countless occasions to discover the source of the noise. Whenever he arrived, the place was always dark and still. The windows were shut, there were no signs of animals, and Roy was living alone in the house. Yet, as soon as he returned downstairs, the nocturnal sounds started up again. "There was no doubt about it," he stated. "It sounded just like there was a whole group of people up there, whispering and whispering about something all night long."

Relentlessly, the ghosts of men, women, and even children returned every night to the attic of the house in Black's Woods. There they whispered to each other for hours on end, finally quieting down in the early hours before sunrise. Finally, Roy had enough. Either he would solve the mystery, or he would have to move out of this maddening house. He contacted a former resident and learned that the whispering had been going on for decades. The previous occupant had also heard the whispering wraiths, who darkened his childhood in the 1980s. This individual told Roy that members of his family sometimes saw the apparition of an old lady rocking relentlessly in a chair at an attic window.

With all this in his head, Roy returned home, vowing to search the attic. The dusty place was filled with furniture, boxes, and chests belonging to people who had once lived in the house. Hoping to find some clues to the hauntings, Roy started rummaging around. He began his search in the area where the whispering seemed most concentrated. After some time, Roy reached the really old belongings, tucked deep under one of the sloping eaves. A steamer trunk at the very back contained three framed pictures—early daguerreotypes. One picture depicted a group of men, women, and children standing at the seashore. An ominous feeling seemed to hang over the whole group, and deep shadows covered the people's eyes. The other two pictures depicted old wooden sailing ships. In the same steamer trunk was a brittle, yellowed business card stating, "Wass, Warren, captain of the barque *Nellie Chapin*." The very last thing Roy found in the old chest was a large china platter in a design called Blue Willow.

This blue-and-white pattern of Chinese motifs is famous worldwide. An elaborate border surrounds a landscape of pagodas, people crossing a bridge, and a little boat sailing to a distant shore. A large willow tree in the center of the design gives the name to the pattern, originally crafted in the 1790s. While the images seem to tell a story, the message is not clear, and the pictures themselves do not come from Chinese mythology or folklore. At any rate, the big, heavy platter found by Roy was impressive, and by all appearances it was well over a hundred years old. Drawn to the objects for their antique value and maritime appearance, Roy brought the platter and photographs downstairs. As soon as he took away the platter and pictures, he never again heard the whispering in the attic. Yet the haunting experiences in the house were far from over, for the contents of the trunk were intimately linked to the haunting experiences at the house.

Roy hung up the old pictures, and thereafter nothing he did could keep them straight. It wasn't that the old photographs were a little crooked—they constantly sloped violently off center. Other pictures hung on the same wall did not shift whatsoever. The catalyst was the Blue Willow platter. One day, Roy brought out the antique dish and placed it on a small table below the pictures of the sailing ships and the people standing at the seashore. When Roy stepped back to look at the ensemble, he was not prepared for what he saw. All at once, right in front of him, the three pictures moved by themselves. They all shifted at the same time and hung there, completely crooked, almost upside down, before his unbelieving eyes. The ghostly manifestations in the house had clearly moved from sound to touch. Even stranger were the events that followed. In the morning, Roy discovered his platter lying broken in half on the floor. The three pictures from the steamer trunk were all also lying strewn on the floor. The homeowner was more than mystified. He was deeply disturbed and threatened by the ghostly occurrences, for no living hand had disturbed his possessions. The house was locked tight from the inside, and nothing else in the house was touched.

Perhaps it was his stubborn streak, or perhaps it was his burning desire to get to the cause of the troubles, but Ray became insistent that the pictures and platter remain exactly where he had placed them. That afternoon, he glued the platter together and returned it to the table. He hung the photographs back on the wall, but in the morning he found everything as it was the day before. The spirits had smashed the platter again, now into many pieces. The old daguerreotypes were also strewn face up on the floor. This happened three times. Roy would glue the platter and hang up the pictures, only to find them on the floor the next day, the dish shattered again and again. Finally, Roy collected all the pieces of the platter and buried them outside on his property. As soon as he did this, the hauntings at the old house came to an abrupt end.

The secret to this baffling series of events can be found in a little-known history of Down East Maine. This is the sad tale of the Palestine Emigration, which took place in 1866, when one hundred and seventy-five people sailed from Jonesport, Maine, to start an evangelical colony in the Holy Land. Their destination was Jaffa. The group included people from Jonesport, Jonesboro, Addison, and a host of other coastal communities. They were caught up in the spell of a traveling evangelist named George Adams. Adams knew the Bible inside out, and was an eloquent speaker. Before long he had started a "great awakening" in Eastern Maine. At the height of revivalism, Adams convinced his followers to sell their property and found a colony in Palestine. Despite heated opposition, a large group of people put their lives, their faith, and their hard-earned money in the man and his dreams.

In Jaffa, the people realized they had been sadly deceived. Adams took to drinking, and the land he promised never materialized. In great suffering, the people languished for months on the burning shores, begging for their livelihood. Disease swept some of them away. Others eventually wandered off in a delirium, never to be seen again. Starvation, of course, kept picking its way through the scattered crowd. Great dissension and disagreement further weakened the people. By spring, the expedition was abandoned, and survivors were making their separate ways back to the coast of Maine. Many never made it back, and those who did carried lifelong burdens of guilt and regret. Though terrible, it is true that some people from this holy crusade were left dying at the gates of Jaffa.

This tragic history goes back to the contents of the steamer trunk discovered in Roy's attic. One of the sailing vessels shown in the old pictures was the *Nellie Chapin*, the actual ship that carried the original expedition to Palestine. Warren Wass, the name on the yellowed business card, was the captain of the *Chapin*. The group of men, women, and children standing at the seashore in Jonesport were all members of the doomed mission. These objects from the old trunk belonged to an occupant of the house who had survived the expedition to Palestine.

Mystery surrounds this person, but clues point to a mad woman we'll call Lavinia. Stephen Madden owned the house at the time of the Palestine Emigration, but neither his name nor those of his immediate family members appear in the list of passengers to Jaffa. Lavinia was either a distant relation or a housekeeper, but she came to live with the Maddens around 1867, and she stayed until her death. Apparently, she spent her last years in isolation, as her mental health deteriorated. Even before this time, Lavinia was psychologically scarred by the trauma of her experiences in Jaffa, but as she grew older, she must have gone insane with her single-minded fixation on the past. Suggesting that she was eventually confined to the attic, Lavinia's spirit returned after death, appearing as an old woman rocking back and forth relentlessly in front of a window on the top floor of the house. This window is located in the immediate vicinity of the old steamer trunk that contained the pictures and the Blue Willow platter.

Blue Willow—its insidious design certainly symbolized the ill-fated expedition. Although the motif is Chinese, the pattern easily lent itself to the doomed Palestine Emigration for the old woman, who obsessively relived her ordeal. The images of people crossing a bridge and a boat sailing to a distant shore represent a trip or expedition. The weeping willow, of course, adds a funereal tone. The pattern on the platter might have served as a psychic trigger, a device upon which the mad woman fixated as she rocked back and forth in the shadows of the old attic.

Somehow Lavinia called up the ghosts of the expedition and channeled the restless spirits into the platter. Strange as this may sound, many accounts exist of psychics conjuring ghosts into crystal balls, mirrors, and other glass or porcelain objects. Some people channel spirits without even realizing it, and perhaps Lavinia, in her madness, was one of these. Staring at the Blue Willow platter, she rocked back and forth, dredging up the past and all the people who died on that doomed expedition.

The ghosts she called up returned as a group to the attic in the Black's Woods, where these spirits once whispered all night long. Trapped in a porcelain tomb, the ghosts literally haunted the Blue Willow platter. Finally demanding a release from their torment, these ghosts smashed that platter for the last time.

20
OLD MAN'S BEARD

rawling out of this twisted ghost tale are the horrors of our worst nightmares: a shocking discovery that confirms the night terror of a child, a foul murder, and the vengeful spirit of a terrible man trapped in a rotting corpse. He is the dead trader of 1633, and he lives among the lichen of the Northeast, the misty, coastal forests steeped in history and blood.

The setting is Clark's Point in Machiasport. By all appearances, it is the best place in the world to raise a child—a quiet dead-end road out on a peninsula of meadows and spruce forests, all surrounded by the glittering blue waters of Machias Bay. But for a young child and his family, the scenery only masked a black pit of fear. For the dead trader had returned from the grave. His purpose remains most inscrutable.

The tale concerns a boy we'll call Tempest, who was seven years old at the time of the manifestation, July 1999. On a moonless, windy night, the boy had trouble falling asleep. Barely perceptible below the rustling of the leaves outside his window stirred the sounds of something creeping around the house. A growing feeling of ill ease and alarm engulfed the boy, who lay wide awake and trembling in his bed under the shadowy eaves of his room.

The terrifying apparition appeared in the least expected place. After a long time, Tempest could stand his ordeal no more and, tossing back the covers, he got up, determined to seek solace in his parents' room, located below on the first floor of the house. Their room contains a set of windows on the south side, and these were directly facing the boy as he opened the door and entered. And that was where he saw the ghost, hovering in one of the windows.

The child stared in a trance of terror at the figure in the window. Chest-high outside the glass was an old man. He looked like a person from long ago, with long hair and a straggling gray beard. Except for a dark vest, the man was bare chested. A terrible thing about the whole apparition was its corpse-like character, for the old man was nothing but a rotting cadaver. But that was not the worst.

Most fearful of all were the eyes. Unlike the dead body of the specter, its eyes were most damnably alive. That was the appalling thing. They were fierce in the intensity of their life force. The eyes also expressed a most evil nature. The old man's eyes turned and fixed malevolently upon the terrified boy. Try as he might, Tempest could not look away or even close his own eyes. He was frozen in fear. To this day, Tempest shudders violently when he recalls those horrible unblinking eyes flashing at him from the face of a corpse.

While time seemed to stop as the spirit stared at him, Tempest was somehow able to break out of the spell long enough to look away and yell at the top of his lungs. In its sheer intensity, this call for help was unlike any his parents had heard before. Certain features of the incident spurred an investigation, which led to surprising results. The boy's terror was strange because he was wide awake, so his shock hadn't resulted from a nightmare. Also strange was the placement of the figure he had seen. Anyone outside the window would have to be floating in the air to appear chest high. Finally, the child's description of the figure was noteworthy, suggestive of a kind of pirate, but not one depicted in any Hollywood movie.

Knowing that Clark's Point has a long history of French and English occupation, Tempest's father, Jason, did some research on the area. This led him to the discovery that it was the site of a trading post established in the seventeenth century by Richard Vines and five other Englishmen. A deadly battle had taken place here with the French, who controlled the region and did not look kindly upon the English incursion.

Of the traders, two were desperate fellows. Warrants stood for their arrest on charges of assault and murder. The men did not live long enough to go to trial for their crimes. They both died when the French commander, La Tour, discovered the trading post in July of 1633. The French were ready for a fight even before they knew that two suspected murderers were working at the post. The rough dwelling stood on a bluff overlooking the shore with a glimpse between the islands to the open sea. Entering the place, La Tour's men apprehended the criminals and shot them on the spot. The other Englishmen departed as hostages of the French, who confiscated the bundles of skins and other goods at the post, valued at 500£. Thus ended the short and bloody history of the trading post in Machiasport.

The location of the trading post corresponds to an ancient cellar hole still located on the south shores of Clark's Point. And to these ruins, Jason went late one day near the end of summer, just after he had learned the terrible history of the place. To get to the ruins, he followed Clark's Point Road all the way up to a trail on the right used by clammers and hikers along Larrabee Cove. Near the beginning of the path, on the left, or ocean side, are the ruins. Although hidden by shrubs and alders, the gaping hole is plainly evident if one takes the time to look.

Oddly enough, a dead spruce tree stands from one of the sides of the cellar hole, and on its sun-bleached branches grows a strange specimen of coastal lichen called old man's beard. Maine's version of Spanish moss, old man's beard adds a gloomy and mysterious atmosphere to the forests along the coast. Normally the lichen grows only a few inches, yet the old man's beard at the site of the trading post is two or three times longer than this, draping a whole branch of the tree. To Jason, the long, straggling lichen was certainly reminiscent of the apparition his son had seen.

Standing in the half light near the dismal ruins of the trading post, Jason could not help wondering if that apparition was the spirit of one of the dead traders. Certainly, everything pointed to that conclusion, including the appearance of the specter, its evil character, and even the time of year. But why did it show up a half mile away, at Tempest's house, and not here? The answer may lie in the time Tempest had spent at the site of the trading post earlier that summer, when he played shadow with his older brother, who had received a metal detector for his birthday. In their travels over Clark's Point, combing the beaches, they searched around the old cellar hole. Perhaps the dead trader is a spirit that follows some people home, especially if they spend too much time at the site of his death. At any rate, it seemed like Tempest had woken something up, the vengeful spirit of the dead trader.

"There were always unresolved questions," Jason later stated. "Since two Englishmen died at the trading post, why did Tempest see only one man? And why was it that the ghost chose to appear as a rotting corpse with living eyes?" Any answers to Jason's questions are speculative at best, but one possibility, which did not occur to him at the time, points to the most disturbing aspect of this whole affair. It concerns the mechanics of digging a grave in the dense forest and rocky ground of Machiasport. The French were likely to be in a great hurry to leave with their hostages, and did not want to waste time breaking new ground. The only reasonable place of burial was the actual cellar of the trading post.

Unthinkable as it may be, the possibility exists that one of the men was still alive when buried there. This alone might explain why only one apparition appeared to Tempest. Perhaps the ghost took the form of a rotting corpse with living eyes to signify the horror of a man who was still alive as the clods of dirt fell upon his bloody face and open eyes.

No one will ever know the depths of true horror lurking unseen along the maze-like coastline of Down East Maine, but the spirit of the dead trader of 1633 stands out as an apparition to avoid at all costs. The ghost of this murderous man haunts the very clay in the cellar hole, where the mossy Old Man's Beard is reflected on black standing waters. One must exercise extreme caution around the cellar hole, as it can be a dangerous pit that fills with water at certain times of the year. Even more risky may be the length of time spent at the place. Be careful not to wake up this vengeful spirit, causing it to appear outside your window in the dead of some windy night.

21
PICTURE ROCKS

Few people know that Down East Maine contains some of the oldest ghost stories in the world. These chilling tales go back more than three thousand years and concern close encounters with the dead. The records also attest to contact with spirits not of human origin. These ghost stories come from the Machias Bay region, located an hour and a half east of Mount Desert Island. Even today, Machias Bay seems shrouded in the other world, with its vast untouched shoreline of inlets, clam flats, peninsulas, and granite cliffs. More striking are the area's picture rocks. These are the stones that tell stories. The tales reveal a record of terrifying phantoms from the mists of time.

The region was an ancient ceremonial center, a place of strange interactions with the spirit world. Attesting to its status as an epicenter of the paranormal, the Machias Bay area contains an extraordinary number of petroglyphs—picture rocks—carved into the ledges. There are more petroglyphs around Machias Bay than anywhere else on the eastern seaboard of the United States. More than five hundred images dot the islands and coastline of Machias Bay. The images appear in at least nine locations around the haunted harbor. Investing the place with a sacred quality, the pictures on the rocks tell prehistoric stories about the supernatural.

Owing to their age and the erosion by rising tides, these images can be difficult to see. Be respectful of the pictures, which are an extremely fragile national heritage. Since petroglyphs are literally pecked into the rocks, look for pictures that have a slightly ragged outline. The pictures will look different from the straight cracks and breaks of natural erosion. Petroglyphs appear best in early morning and late afternoon. Without shadows, the images are virtually invisible. Of course, seeing the petroglyphs also depends on the ocean. Most of these images are under water twice a day at high tide.

When the rocks reveal themselves, they depict a story written out in the form of pictures. The difficulty in finding these images is part of the experience, making the long-awaited sighting an almost mystical experience. To this day, people continue to discover new petroglyphs around the area. A ghostly image is invisible one moment, and the next minute, when the light changes, the picture jumps out from the surface, never to appear again so clearly for a hundred years. Seeing the images becomes a kind of ghostly encounter. The trace of someone dead for thousands of years reappears to tell a strange tale. The storytellers are like phantoms, and so are the petroglyphs they made, which form a bridge between one world and another.

Called "pictures of the devil" by early settlers—and dismissed as prehistoric graffiti by modern people—the petroglyphs are actually sacred images belonging to the region's First Peoples, and their descendents, the Passamaquoddy. The time-worn pictures on the sea ledges come from a culture saturated in the spirit world, a society centered on the role of a shaman—called a *medeulin*—who negotiated with the spirit world. Shamans designed the imagery pecked onto the rocks by apprentices. In chants and songs, the Indians then retold the ghost stories illustrated in the images on the rocks. Well into the late eighteenth century, huge gatherings were still taking place around the picture rocks of Machias Bay. In one location, more than two hundred birch-bark canoes were moored while bonfires blazed throughout the night, ringing with chants and drums.

The picture rocks depict the spirits of the living and the dead. Some human figures appear headless, and these are the spirits of the deceased. They have no heads because they communicate only in dreams and trance states. These specters usually appear to the left of anything alive. Pictures of moose, deer, and caribou leap from the rocks, but these are not the representations of living game. They are pictures of the spirits of the animals. The human hunters that sometimes appear in these scenes are also spirits, the souls of the hunters. The idea was to make some kind of negotiation in the spirit world that would bring about a successful hunt. In some of the torsos of human figures there appears a vertical line, an image of the soul inside the body.

Ominous indeed are the old stories of demonic possession. The rocky ledges around Machias Bay contain a number of images representing ghosts inhabiting the bodies of the living. A possessed person appears as a figure with one head but four legs. In some cases, these pictures show shamans acting as psychic mediums channeling the spirits of the dead. In other instances, the pictures show demons possessing people. For the Native Americans who migrated here every fall, dangerous entities lurked in the vicinity. The waterfalls of Machias, located three miles inland from the bay, was an evil place, shunned by early Native Americans. The legacy of the place even appears the name of Machias—bad little falls. Certainly, Algonquin lore contains many terrifying entities. Some peroglyphs depict evil spirits inhabiting human victims.

In pictures on the ledges, some dreaded ghosts represent entities not of human origin. Besides animal spirits, tiny ghostly figures often appear, usually dancing around the image of a shaman. These are spirit familiars, which are friendly. Others phantoms nearby are dangerous, even life threatening. In one instance, a monstrous water spirit rears its head. In another, a human stands with the head of a bird of prey. Even apparently innocent images become ominous when examined in relation to other pictures. Parallel arcs show paths to the spirit world. If the arcs don't return, then they lead to a place of darkness. A picture of a sixteenth-century European sailing vessel includes arcing spirit lines that don't return, suggesting that the vessel was evil, a kind of black hole.

One of the most sinister stories of the petroglyphs concerns a moth-like phantom. This ghost hovers over a group of four humans bound together on the shore. The image is tantalizing and suggests the record of an ancient supernatural sighting on these very shores. Perhaps it even depicts people preyed upon by a strange inhuman entity. No matter what, the petroglyphs offer a stern warning for all who see them. On these shores, one must beware, for terrifying forces inhabit the lonely byways.

Around Machias Bay, contemporary accounts of supernatural wonders continue a story begun more than three thousand years ago. With regularity over the years, people report strange lights and sounds that concentrate on the shore. Black silhouettes that stalk the twilight have terrified residents for hundreds of years. From Machias Bay come sightings of strange animals—such a white roe buck—and strange humans with animal-like features—like a man with cloven feet. Such accounts clearly resemble some of the stone images on the shores nearby. Most horrifying of all is a ghost that haunts the beaches around the petroglyphs. This phantom strikes terror in all who encounter it. Although it thrives at night, it can appear in the day, and it moves with startling speed. The creature's cry is a ghastly inhalation of air. In a kind of mad fury, the phantom returns through time to stalk the mystic shoreline.

And so these shores live up to their terrifying spiritual heritage. In records going back to the dawn of time, ghostly encounters take place in the coastal shadows of Down East Maine. The Native Americans called the place *Squasadek*, meaning the waiting and watching place. It was a place to watch for spirits. And it is still a place to find them.

References

Abbreviations

ML-Marcus LiBrizzi
UMM-University of Maine at Machias

Chapter 1: Phantoms of Ledgelawn

Levin, Robert. "The Ghost of Ledgelawn." *Mount Desert Islander.*
Vol. 7. No. 43. 2007. 1, 11.

From fieldwork collections by ML: interview with Jomar Castro,
June 2007 and June 2009; interview with Mike Gallant, June 2007
and 13 February 2009; interview with Sherry Gallant, June 2007
and 13 February 2009; interview with Gerda Ferreira, 9 January
2010; interview with Fatima Oliveira 14 January 2010.

Chapter 2: Acts of the Unspeakable

"The Corsair's Retreat: A Story of the Slave Trade." *Mount Desert
Herald.* 21 June 1883. 1.

Kelly, Robin G. G. and Earl Lewis. *To Make Our World Anew: A
History of African-Americans to 1880.* New York: Oxford University
Press, 2000.

From fieldwork collections by ML: interviews with Jim Maren,
October 2007 and July 2009.

Chapter 3: Horror at Bass Harbor Head Light

D'Entremont, Jeremy. "Bass Harbor Light." New England's
Lighthouses: A Virtual Tour. http://lighthouse.cc/bassharbor/
history.html, 22 March 2007.

Harrison, Timothy E. *Lighthouses of Bar Harbor and the Acadia Region.* Images of America. Bar Harbor: Acadia Publishing, 2009.

Welton, Dianne, interviewed by Andrea Memmelaar, 12 April 1967, Maine Folklife Center, University of Maine, Archive 302.

From fieldwork collections by ML: telephone interviews with Dianne Welton Meder and Dorothy Meyer, October 2009.

Chapter 4: The Shore Path

Byran, John M. and Richard Cheek. *Maine Cottages: Fred Savage and the Architecture of Mount Desert.* New York: Princeton Architectural, 2005.

Gray, T.M. *Ghosts of Maine.* Atglen: Schiffer, 2008.

Perrin, Steve. *The Shore Path.* Bar Harbor: Earthling, 2000.

Mrs. Alton Woodworth, interviewed by Roger Woodworth, 26 November 1966. Maine Folklife Center, University of Maine, Archive 433.

From fieldwork collections by ML and UMM Students: Daisy Harper, interviewed by the author 17 July 2009 and 29 August 2009; Bobbie Lynn Hutchins, Suzanne Becque, and Sabin Hutchins, interviewed by the author 14 September 2009; Zilah Silva, interviewed by the author 28 December 2009; David Marino, account submitted 30 September 2004.

Chapter 5: Shadows from the Flames

Butler, Joyce. *Wildfire Loose: The Week That Maine Burned.* Kennebunkport, ME: Durrell, n.d.

Heath, John and David Sleeper. *The Bar Harbor Fire.* Pamphlet published by the *Bar Harbor Times,* 1947.

Schulte, Carol Olivieri. *Ghosts on the Coast of Maine*. Camden, ME: Down East Books, 1989.

Street, George E. *Mount Desert: A History*. 1905. Boston: Houghton, 1926.

From fieldwork collections by ML and UMM students: Daisy Harper, interviewed by the author, 17 July 2009; Sabin Hutchins, interviewed by the author, 14 September 2009; Patrick Roy, account submitted 6 November 2008; Joshua Poulin, account submitted 6 November 2008.

Chapter 6: A Phantom in the Turrets

Lincoln, Nan. "The Turrets Turns 100." *Bar Harbor Times*. 21 September 1995. B1–B2.

"The Turrets: A Restored Reminder of a Vanished Way of Life." *Summer Times*. September 1983. 12, 16.

"Beautiful Grounds: A Description of the Emery Cottage and Surroundings." *Bar Harbor Record*. 5 June 1985.

Parr, William. "'Everything was Perfect at the Turrets." 1971. *Bar Harbor Times*. 14 November.

From fieldwork collections by ML: Interviews with students from College of the Atlantic, 2 October 2009 and 16 October 2009.

Chapter 7: The Creeping at Seal Cove

Leland, Nelson, interviewed by Roger Woodworth, 6 November 1966. Maine Folklife Center, University of Maine, Archive 433.

Vandenbergh, Lydia Bodman. *Revisiting Seal Harbor and Acadia National Park*. Dover, NH: Arcadia, 1996.

Biard, Pierre. *Relation of the St. Saveur Colony*. Reprinted with translation in R.G. Thwaites, ed. *Jesuit Relations*, III, IV. Cleveland: Burrows, 1897.

"A Famous Field: Historic Reminiscences about Mount Desert." *Mount Desert Herald*. 15 August 1884. 1.

Gray, T.M. *Ghosts of Maine*. Atglen: Schiffer, 2008.

"The Grotto of Mount Desert: An Old-Time Mystery." *Mount Desert Herald*. 15 February 1883. 1.

"Legends of Mount Desert: Part Fourth—The Smuggler's Cave." *Mount Desert Herald*. 14 August 1885. 1.

"Mount Desert: Incidents of Its Discovery and Settlement." *Mount Desert Herald*. 13 August 1881. 1.

"Mount Desert: Incidents of Its Discovery and Settlement: Part 3." *Mount Desert Herald*. 17 August 1881. 1.

Schulte, Carol Olivieri. *Ghosts on the Coast of Maine*. Camden, ME: Down East Books, 1989.

St. Germain, Tom and Jay Saunders. *Trails of History: The Story of Mount Desert Island's Paths from Norembega to Acadia*. Bar Harbor: Parkman, 1993.

"St. Saveur: Early Settlement of Southwest Harbor." 1882. *Bar Harbor Herald*. 18 August.

Thornton, Mrs. Seth S. *Traditions and Records of Southwest Harbor and Somesville, Mount Desert Island, Maine*. Somesville, ME, 1938.

Chapter 9: Witchcraft at Southwest Harbor

O.H.F. "Kidd's Treasure: Is It Buried at Fernald Point?" *Mount Desert Herald.* 22 August 1882. 1.

Smallidge, Robert, interviewed by Richard Lunt, 28 September 1963. Maine Folklife Center, University of Maine, Archive 2970.

Thornton, Mrs. Seth S. *Traditions and Records of Southwest Harbor and Somesville, Mount Desert Island, Maine.* Somesville, ME, 1938.

From fieldwork collections by ML: interview with Freya Elizabeth Gallagher, 11 July 2007 and 17 July 2009; interview with Daisy Harper, 17 July 2009.

Chapter 10: Bar Harbor Club

"The Bar Harbor Club 50th Anniversary." Bar Harbor: Bar Harbor Club. 24 July 1980.

Boyer-Basso, Becky. "After 20 Years Bar Harbor Club Open to Public." *Mount Desert Islander.* 23 June 2005. 1.

Photograph, circa 1900. "Devil's Half Acre." Bar Harbor Historical Society Archives.

"The New Bar Harbor Club." *Bar Harbor Times.* 28 April 1988. c1–c3.

Phippen, Stanford. "When the Bar Harbor Club Ruled the Town." *Out and About in Downeast Maine.* September 2005. 9, 55.

From fieldwork collections by ML and UMM students: Freya Gallagher, interviewed by the author 17 July 2009, Adam N. Hilton, interviewed by Josh Poulin 18 September 2008: Meghan Bishop and Maegin Mccue, interviewed by the author 4 August 2007.

Chapter 11: The Curse of Schooner Head

"Legend of Schooner Head." *Bar Harbor Record*. 24 July 1885.

Garrett, Edwin Atleee III. "Unromantic as Monday Morning." Bar Harbor Historical Society Papers. 2003.

Gracie, Archibald. Chapter 2: "Struck by an Iceberg." *The Truth about the Titanic*. 1913. Riverside, CT: 7 C's Press, 1973.

Lapham, William Berry. *Bar Harbor and Mount Desert Island*. Augusta: Maine Farmer Job, 1886.

Marshall, Logan. *Sinking of the Titanic and Great Sea Disasters*. Philadelphia: Winston, 1912.

Stover, Isabelle and Kathryn Mittelberger. "History of High Seas." 16 August 1974. Bar Harbor Historical Society Papers.

"Sudden Death of Prof. Brunnow." *Bar Harbor Times and Record*. 21 April 1917. 1.

Chapter 12: Haunting at Compass Harbor

Dorr, George B. *The Story of Acadia National Park*. Books I and II. 1942, 1948, posthumously. Bar Harbor: Acadia Publishing, 1985.

Goldstein, Judith S. *Tragedies and Triumphs: The Founding of Acadia National Park*. Somesville, ME: Port in a Storm, 1992.

National Park Service. "George B. Dorr." U.S. Department of Interior. www.nps.gov/acad/historyculture/george-b-dorr.htm.

"George Dorr Makes a Gift to Acadia Park." *Bar Harbor Times*. 15 January 1942.

"Wharton at Oldfarm." *Bar Harbor Times and Record*. 18 August 1917.

Chapter 13: Ghosts from the Back Side

Morison, Samuel Eliot. *The Story of Mount Desert Island.* Boston: Little Brown, 1960.

From fieldwork collections by ML and UMM students: Linda Graham, interviewed by Dan Clossen, 11 October 2009, and interviewed by the author on 26 October 2009.

Chapter 14: Wreck of the *Grand Design*

Hale, Richard Walden Jr. *The Story of Bar Harbor: An Informal History Recording One Hundred and Fifty Years in the Life of a Community.* New York: Washburn, 1949.

Eaton, Cyrus. *Annals of the Town of Warren, in Knox County, Maine.* Boston: Masters and Livermore, 1877.

Street, George E. *Mount Desert: A History.* 1905. Boston: Houghton, 1926.

"Wreck of the Grand Design." Bar Harbor Times. 5 May 1988, 1.

Chapter 15: The Gates to Hell

Brechlin, Earl. *Bygone Bar Harbor: A Postcard Tour of MDI and Acadia National Park.* Camden, ME: Down East Books, 2002.

Drake, Samuel Adams. *The Pine-Tree State.* Boston: Estes and Lauriat. 1891.

"The Ovens: Legends of Mount Desert, Part Fifth." *Mount Desert Herald.* 25 August 1885. 1.

Chapter 16: The Proving Ground

Speck, Frank G. *Penobscot Shamanism.* Millwood, NY: Kraus, 1974.

Jonas Crane, interviewed by Zelda Havey and Ivy Young, 14 October 1963. Maine Folklife Center, University of Maine, Archive 182.

From fieldwork collections by ML and UMM Students: ML interviews with Alex Whitney, Daroll Whitney, Linda Whitney, Tina Whitney, Betty Williams, 27 July 2009; Derik Lee, interview with Alex Whitney, 14 February 2007.

Chapter 17: A Face in the Water
"Haunted History: Haunted Maine." *The History Channel*. A&E Television Networks. Written and directed by Tom Jennings. 2001.

Hearn, Lafcadio. *Oriental Ghost Stories*. Hertfordshire: Wordsworth, 2007.

Leach, Cheryl. *Echoes of the Past*. Philadelphia: Xlibris, 2004.

"Sarah Ware: About Her Head." *The Enterprise*. Vol. 7. No. 32. 20 August 1998. 1.

Spooner, Emeric. *In Search of Sarah Ware: Reinvestigating Murder and Conspiracy in a Maine Village*. Create Space, Charleston, SC: 2009.

From fieldwork collections by UMM student: Adam Brown, account submitted 13 February 2007.

Chapter 18: The Return of Hate Evil

History of Jonesboro, Maine, 1809–2009. 2009. *Collaboration of Bicentennial Committee*. 2009.

"A Genealogical Relic." *Bulletin of the Maine State Library*. 1–6. Maine Library Commission. Maine State Library. April 1913. Vol. 2. No. 4. 2–3.

From fieldwork collections by ML: interview with Bethany Foss, Linda Patryn, and Jessica Mace, 18 February 2010.

Chapter 19: Blue Willow

Drake, Samuel Adams. *The Pine-Tree State*. Boston: Estes and Lauriat. 1891.

Federal Writers Project. *Maine: A Guide 'Down East.'* Boston: Houghton Mifflin, 1937.

Holmes, Reed. *The Forerunners*. 1981. 2nd edition with epilogue by Jean L. Holmes. Pepperell, MA: Holmes, 2003.

Mitchell and Campbell. *The Jonesport Register*. Brunswick, ME: Mitchell, 1905.

From fieldwork collections by ML: interview with Roy Montana, 9 February 2008.

Chapter 20: Old Man's Beard

Varney, George J. 1886. *History of Machias, Maine: From A Gazetteer of the State of Maine*. Boston: B.B. Russell.

Winthrop, John. *The Journal of John Winthrop, 1630–1649*. Eds. Richard S. Dunn, James Savage, and Laetitia Yeandle. Cambridge: Belknap, 1996.

Chapter 21: Picture Rocks

Lentik, Edward J. "Machias Bay Petroglyphs." *Picture Rocks: American Indian Rock Art in the Northeast Woodlands*. Lebanon, NH: University Press of New England, 2002.

Song of the Drum: The Petroglyphs of Maine. Ray Gerbin, producer and director, Mark Hedd writer. Acadia Productions. 47 min. 2004.

From fieldwork collections by ML: interview with residents of Machiasport, July 2007.

Photographic Credits

Photographs for this book were taken in 2009 and 2010
at the actual locations specified by the tales.

Photographs by Marcus LiBrizzi:
> Phantoms of Ledgelawn
> Acts of the Unspeakable
> Horror at Bass Harbor Head Light
> Shadows from the Flames
> The Creeping at Seal Cove
> The Sinister Web of 1613
> The Bar Harbor Club
> Haunting at Compass Harbor
> Wreck of the *Grand Design*
> The Gates to Hell
> The Proving Ground
> Blue Willow
> Old Man's Beard
> Picture Rocks

Photographs by Daisy Harper, of *Paper-Mâché Dream Photography*:
> A Phantom in the Turrets
> Witchcraft at Southwest Harbor
> The Curse of Schooner Head
> Ghosts from the Back Side

Photographs by Audrey May Dufour, of *Audrey May Photography*:
> The Shore Path
> A Face in the Water
> The Return of Hate Evil

Special thanks go out to Michael Matis for
editorial assistance and to Daisy Harper
for her time and vision in preparing the
photographs in this volume for publication.